Saul Bellow

Mosby's Memoirs
and
Other Stories

PENGUIN BOOKS

Penguin Books Ltd, Harmondsworth,
Middlesex, England
Penguin Books, 625 Madison Avenue,
New York, New York 10022, U.S.A.
Penguin Books Australia Ltd, Ringwood,
Victoria, Australia
Penguin Books Canada Limited, 2801 John Street,
Markham, Ontario, Canada L3R 1B4
Penguin Books (N.Z.) Ltd, 182–190 Wairau Road,
Auckland 10, New Zealand

First published in the United States of America by
The Viking Press 1968
Published in Penguin Books 1977

ISBN 0 14 00.4524 4

Printed in the United States of America by
Offset Paperback Mfrs., Inc., Dallas, Pennsylvania
Set in Linotype Primer

"Looking for Mr. Green" originally appeared in *Commentary;*
"The Gonzaga Manuscripts" in *Discovery No. 4;*
"Leaving the Yellow House" in *Esquire;*
"A Father-to-Be" and "Mosby's Memoirs"
in *The New Yorker;*
and "The Old System" in *Playboy.*

CONTENTS

Leaving the Yellow House (1957)   3

The Old System (1967)   43

Looking for Mr. Green (1951)   85

The Gonzaga Manuscripts (1954)   111

A Father-to-Be (1955)   143

Mosby's Memoirs (1968)   157

MOSBY'S MEMOIRS
AND OTHER STORIES

LEAVING THE YELLOW HOUSE

The neighbors—there were in all six white people who lived at Sego Desert Lake—told one another that old Hattie could no longer make it alone. The desert life, even with a forced-air furnace in the house and butane gas brought from town in a truck, was still too difficult for her. There were women even older than Hattie in the county. Twenty miles away was Amy Walters, the gold miner's widow. But she was a hardier old girl. Every day of the year she took a bath in the icy lake. And Amy was crazy about money and knew how to manage it, as Hattie did not. Hattie was not exactly a drunkard, but she hit the bottle pretty hard, and now she was in trouble and there was a limit to the help she could expect from even the best of neighbors.

They were fond of her, though. You couldn't help being fond of Hattie. She was big and cheerful, puffy, comic, boastful, with a big round back and stiff, rather long legs. Before the century began she had graduated from finishing school and studied the organ in Paris. But now she didn't know a note from a skillet. She had tantrums when she played canasta. And all that remained of her fine fair hair was frizzled along her forehead in small gray curls. Her forehead was not much wrinkled, but the skin was bluish, the color of skim milk. She walked with long strides in spite of the heaviness of her hips, pushing on, roundbacked, with her shoulders and showing the flat rubber bottoms of her shoes.

Once a week, in the same cheerful, plugging but absent way, she took off her short skirt and the dirty aviator's jacket with the wool collar and put on a girdle, a dress, and high-heeled shoes. When she stood on these heels her fat old body trembled. She wore a big brown Rembrandt-like tam with a ten-cent-store brooch, eyelike, carefully centered. She drew a straight line with lipstick on her mouth, leaving part of the upper lip pale. At the wheel of her old turret-shaped car, she drove, seemingly methodical but speeding dangerously, across forty miles of mountainous desert to buy frozen meat pies and whisky. She went to the laundromat and the hairdresser, and then had lunch with two martinis at the Arlington. Afterward she would often visit Marian Nabot's Silvermine Hotel at Miller Street near skid row and pass the rest of the day gossiping and drinking with her cronies, old divorcees like herself who had settled in the West. Hattie never gambled any more and she didn't care for the movies. And at five o'clock she drove back at the same speed, calmly, partly blinded by the smoke of her cigarette. The fixed cigarette gave her a watering eye.

The Rolfes and the Paces were her only white neighbors at Sego Desert Lake. There was Sam Jervis too, but he was only an old gandy walker who did odd jobs in her garden, and she did not count him. Nor did she count among her neighbors Darly, the dudes' cowboy who worked for the Paces, nor Swede, the telegrapher. Pace had a guest ranch, and Rolfe and his wife were rich and had retired. Thus there were three good houses at the lake, Hattie's yellow house, Pace's, and the Rolfes'. All the rest of the population —Sam, Swede, Watchtah the section foreman, and the Mexicans and Indians and Negroes—lived in shacks and box-cars. There were very few trees, cottonwoods and box elders. Everything else, down to the shores, was sagebrush and juniper. The lake was what remained of an old sea that had covered the volcanic mountains. To the north there were some tungsten mines; to the south, fifteen miles, was an Indian village—shacks built of plywood or railroad ties.

In this barren place Hattie had lived for more than twenty years. Her first summer was spent not in a house but in an Indian wickiup on the shore. She used to say that she had watched the stars from this almost roofless shelter. After her divorce she took up with a cowboy named Wicks. Neither of them had any money—it was the Depression— and they had lived on the range, trapping coyotes for a living. Once a month they would come into town and rent a room and go on a bender. Hattie told this sadly, but also gloatingly, and with many trimmings. A thing no sooner happened to her than it was transformed into something else. "We were caught in a storm," she said, "and we rode hard, down to the lake and knocked on the door of the yellow house"—now her house. "Alice Parmenter took us in and let us sleep on the floor." What had actually happened was that the wind was blowing—there had been no storm—and they were not far from the house anyway; and Alice Parmenter, who knew that Hattie and Wicks were not married, offered them separate beds; but Hattie, swaggering, had said in a loud voice, "Why get two sets of sheets dirty?" And she and her cowboy had slept in Alice's bed while Alice had taken the sofa.

Then Wicks went away. There was never anybody like him in the sack; he was brought up in a whorehouse and the girls had taught him everything, said Hattie. She didn't really understand what she was saying but believed that she

was being Western. More than anything else she wanted to
be thought of as a rough, experienced woman of the West.
Still, she was a lady, too. She had good silver and good
china and engraved stationery, but she kept canned beans
and A-1 sauce and tuna fish and bottles of catsup and fruit
salad on the library shelves of her living room. On her
night table was the Bible her pious brother Angus—the
other brother was a heller—had given her; but behind the
little door of the commode was a bottle of bourbon. When
she awoke in the night she tippled herself back to sleep. In
the glove compartment of her old car she kept little sample
bottles for emergencies on the road. Old Darly found them
after her accident.

The accident did not happen far out in the desert as she
had always feared, but very near home. She had had a few
martinis with the Rolfes one evening, and as she was driving home over the railroad crossing she lost control of the
car and veered off the crossing onto the tracks. The explanation she gave was that she had sneezed, and the sneeze
had blinded her and made her twist the wheel. The motor
was killed and all four wheels of the car sat smack on the
rails. Hattie crept down from the door, high off the roadbed. A great fear took hold of her—for the car, for the future, and not only for the future but spreading back into
the past—and she began to hurry on stiff legs through the
sagebrush to Pace's ranch.

Now the Paces were away on a hunting trip and had left
Darly in charge; he was tending bar in the old cabin
that went back to the days of the pony express, when Hattie
burst in. There were two customers, a tungsten miner and
his girl.

"Darly, I'm in trouble. Help me. I've had an accident,"
said Hattie.

How the face of a man will alter when a woman has bad
news to tell him! It happened now to lean old Darly; his

eyes went flat and looked unwilling, his jaw moved in and out, his wrinkled cheeks began to flush, and he said, "What's the matter—what's happened to you now?"

"I'm stuck on the tracks. I sneezed. I lost control of the car. Tow me off, Darly. With the pickup. Before the train comes."

Darly threw down his towel and stamped his high-heeled boots. "Now what have you gone and done?" he said. "I told you to stay home after dark."

"Where's Pace? Ring the fire bell and fetch Pace."

"There's nobody on the property except me," said the lean old man. "And I'm not supposed to close the bar and you know it as well as I do."

"Please, Darly. I can't leave my car on the tracks."

"Too bad!" he said. Nevertheless he moved from behind the bar. "How did you say it happened?"

"I told you, I sneezed," said Hattie.

Everyone, as she later told it, was as drunk as sixteen thousand dollars: Darly, the miner, and the miner's girl.

Darly was limping as he locked the door of the bar. A year before, a kick from one of Pace's mares had broken his ribs as he was loading her into the trailer, and he hadn't recovered from it. He was too old. But he dissembled the pain. The high-heeled narrow boots helped, and his painful bending looked like the ordinary stooping posture of a cowboy. However, Darly was not a genuine cowboy, like Pace who had grown up in the saddle. He was a late-comer from the East and until the age of forty had never been on horseback. In this respect he and Hattie were alike. They were not genuine Westerners.

Hattie hurried after him through the ranch yard.

"Damn you!" he said to her. "I got thirty bucks out of that sucker and I would have skinned him out of his whole pay check if you minded your business. Pace is going to be sore as hell."

"You've got to help me. We're neighbors," said Hattie.

"You're not fit to be living out here. You can't do it any more. Besides, you're swacked all the time."

Hattie couldn't afford to talk back. The thought of her car on the tracks made her frantic. If a freight came now and smashed it, her life at Sego Desert Lake would be finished. And where would she go then? She was not fit to live in this place. She had never made the grade at all, only seemed to have made it. And Darly—why did he say such hurtful things to her? Because he himself was sixty-eight years old, and he had no other place to go, either; he took bad treatment from Pace besides. Darly stayed because his only alternative was to go to the soldiers' home. Moreover, the dude women would still crawl into his sack. They wanted a cowboy and they thought he was one. Why, he couldn't even raise himself out of his bunk in the morning. And where else would he get women? "After the dude season," she wanted to say to him, "you always have to go to the Veterans' Hospital to get fixed up again." But she didn't dare offend him now.

The moon was due to rise. It appeared as they drove over the ungraded dirt road toward the crossing where Hattie's turret-shaped car was sitting on the rails. Driving very fast, Darly wheeled the pickup around, spraying dirt on the miner and his girl, who had followed in their car.

"You get behind the wheel and steer," Darly told Hattie.

She climbed into the seat. Waiting at the wheel, she lifted up her face and said, "Please God, I didn't bend the axle or crack the oil pan."

When Darly crawled under the bumper of Hattie's car the pain in his ribs suddenly cut off his breath, so instead of doubling the tow chain he fastened it at full length. He rose and trotted back to the truck on the tight boots. Motion seemed the only remedy for the pain; not even booze did the trick any more. He put the pickup into towing gear and began to pull. One side of Hattie's car dropped into the roadbed with a heave of springs. She sat with a stormy, frightened, conscience-stricken face, racing the motor until she flooded it.

The tungsten miner yelled, "Your chain's too long."

Hattie was raised high in the air by the pitch of the wheels. She had to roll down the window to let herself out because the door handle had been jammed from inside for years. Hattie struggled out on the uplifted side crying, "I better call the Swede. I better have him signal. There's a train due."

"Go on, then," said Darly. "You're no good here."

"Darly, be careful with my car. Be careful."

The ancient sea bed at this place was flat and low, and the lights of her car and of the truck and of the tungsten miner's Chevrolet were bright and big at twenty miles. Hattie was too frightened to think of this. All she could think was that she was a procrastinating old woman, she had lived by delays; she had meant to stop drinking, she had put off the time, and now she had smashed her car—a terrible end, a terrible judgment on her. She got to the ground and, drawing up her skirt, she started to get over the tow chain. To prove that the chain didn't have to be shortened, and to get the whole thing over with, Darly threw the pickup forward again. The chain jerked up and struck Hattie in the knee and she fell forward and broke her arm.

She cried, "Darly, Darly, I'm hurt. I fell."

"The old lady tripped on the chain," said the miner. "Back up here and I'll double it for you. You're getting no-wheres."

Drunkenly the miner lay down on his back in the dark, soft red cinders of the roadbed. Darly had backed up to slacken the chain.

Darly hurt the miner, too. He tore some skin from his fingers by racing ahead before the chain was secure. Without complaining, the miner wrapped his hand in his shirt-tail saying, "She'll do it now." The old car came down from the tracks and stood on the shoulder of the road.

"There's your goddamn car," said Darly to Hattie.

"Is it all right?" she said. Her left side was covered with dirt, but she managed to pick herself up and stand, round-backed and heavy, on her stiff legs. "I'm hurt, Darly." She tried to convince him of it.

"Hell if you are," he said. He believed she was putting on an act to escape blame. The pain in his ribs made him especially impatient with her. "Christ, if you can't look after yourself any more you've got no business out here."

"You're old yourself," she said. "Look what you did to me. You can't hold your liquor."

This offended him greatly. He said, "I'll take you to the Rolfes. They let you booze it up in the first place, so let them worry about you. I'm tired of your bunk, Hattie."

He raced uphill. Chains, spade, and crowbar clashed on the sides of the pickup. She was frightened and held her arm and cried. Rolfe's dogs jumped at her to lick her when she went through the gate. She shrank from them crying, "Down, down."

"Darly," she cried in the darkness, "take care of my car. Don't leave it standing there on the road. Darly, take care of it, please."

But Darly in his ten-gallon hat, his chin-bent face wrinkled, small and angry, a furious pain in his ribs, tore away at high speed.

"Oh, God, what will I do," she said.

The Rolfes were having a last drink before dinner, sitting at their fire of pitchy railroad ties, when Hattie opened the door. Her knee was bleeding, her eyes were tiny with shock, her face gray with dust.

"I'm hurt," she said desperately. "I had an accident. I sneezed and lost control of the wheel. Jerry, look after the car. It's on the road."

They bandaged her knee and took her home and put her to bed. Helen Rolfe wrapped a heating pad around her arm.

"I can't have the pad," Hattie complained. "The switch goes on and off, and every time it does it starts my generator and uses up the gas."

"Ah, now, Hattie," Rolfe said, "this is not the time to be stingy. We'll take you to town in the morning and have you looked over. Helen will phone Dr. Stroud."

Hattie wanted to say, "Stingy! Why you're the stingy ones. I just haven't got anything. You and Helen are ready to hit each other over two bits in canasta." But the Rolfes were good to her; they were her only real friends here. Darly would have let her lie in the yard all night, and Pace would have sold her to the bone man. He'd give her to the knacker for a buck.

So she didn't talk back to the Rolfes, but as soon as they left the yellow house and walked through the super-clear moonlight under the great skirt of box-elder shadows to their new station wagon, Hattie turned off the switch, and the heavy swirling and battering of the generator stopped. Presently she became aware of real pain, deeper pain, in her arm, and she sat rigid, warming the injured place with her hand. It seemed to her that she could feel the bone sticking out. Before leaving, Helen Rolfe had thrown over her a comforter that had belonged to Hattie's dead friend India, from whom she had inherited the small house and everything in it. Had the comforter lain on India's bed the night she died? Hattie tried to remember, but her thoughts were mixed up. She was fairly sure the deathbed pillow was in the loft, and she believed she had put the death bedding in a trunk. Then how had this comforter got out? She couldn't do anything about it now but draw it away from contact with her skin. It kept her legs warm. This she accepted, but she didn't want it any nearer.

More and more Hattie saw her own life as though, from

birth to the present, every moment had been filmed. Her fancy was that when she died she would see the film in the next world. Then she would know how she had appeared from the back, watering the plants, in the bathroom, asleep, playing the organ, embracing—everything, even tonight, in pain, almost the last pain, perhaps, for she couldn't take much more. How many twists and angles had life to show her yet? There couldn't be much film left. To lie awake and think such thoughts was the worst thing in the world. Better death than insomnia. Hattie not only loved sleep, she believed in it.

The first attempt to set the bone was not successful. "Look what they've done to me," said Hattie and showed visitors the discolored breast. After the second operation her mind wandered. The sides of her bed had to be raised, for in her delirium she roamed the wards. She cursed at the nurses when they shut her in. "You can't make people prisoners in a democracy without a trial, you bitches." She had learned from Wicks how to swear. "*He* was profane," she used to say. "I picked it up unconsciously."

For several weeks her mind was not clear. Asleep, her face was lifeless; her cheeks were puffed out and her mouth, no longer wide and grinning, was drawn round and small. Helen sighed when she saw her.

"Shall we get in touch with her family?" Helen asked the doctor. His skin was white and thick. He had chestnut hair, abundant but very dry. He sometimes explained to his patients, "I had a tropical disease during the war."

He asked, "Is there a family?"

"Old brothers. Cousins' children," said Helen. She tried to think who would be called to her own bedside (she was old enough for that). Rolfe would see that she was cared for. He would hire private nurses. Hattie could not afford that. She had already gone beyond her means. A trust company in Philadelphia paid her eighty dollars a month. She had a small savings account.

"I suppose it'll be up to us to get her out of hock," said Rolfe. "Unless the brother down in Mexico comes across. We may have to phone one of those old guys."

In the end, no relations had to be called. Hattie began to recover. At last she could recognize visitors, though her mind was still in disorder. Much that had happened she couldn't recall.

"How many quarts of blood did they have to give me?" she kept asking. "I seem to remember five, six, eight different transfusions. Daylight, electric light . . ." She tried to smile, but she couldn't make a pleasant face as yet. "How am I going to pay?" she said. "At twenty-five bucks a quart. My little bit of money is just about wiped out."

Blood became her constant topic, her preoccupation. She told everyone who came to see her, "—have to replace all that blood. They poured gallons into me. Gallons. I hope it was all good." And, though very weak, she began to grin and laugh again. There was more hissing in her laughter than formerly; the illness had affected her chest.

"No cigarettes, no booze," the doctor told Helen.

"Doctor," Helen asked him, "do you expect her to change?"

"All the same, I am obliged to say it."

"Life sober may not be much of a temptation to her," said Helen.

Her husband laughed. When Rolfe's laughter was intense it blinded one of his eyes. His short Irish face turned red; on the bridge of his small, sharp nose the skin whitened. "Hattie's like me," he said. "She'll be in business till she's cleaned out. And if Sego Lake turned to whisky she'd use her last strength to knock her old yellow house down to build a raft of it. She'd float away on whisky. So why talk temperance?"

Hattie recognized the similarity between them. When he came to see her she said, "Jerry, you're the only one I can really talk to about my troubles. What am I going to do for money? I have Hotchkiss Insurance. I paid eight dollars a month."

"That won't do you much good, Hat. No Blue Cross?"

"I let it drop ten years ago. Maybe I could sell some of my valuables."

"What valuables have you got?" he said. His eye began to droop with laughter.

"Why," she said defiantly, "there's plenty. First there's the beautiful, precious Persian rug that India left me."

"Coals from the fireplace have been burning it for years, Hat!"

"The rug is in *perfect* condition," she said with an angry sway of the shoulders. "A beautiful object like that never loses its value. And the oak table from the Spanish monastery is three hundred years old."

"With luck you could get twenty bucks for it. It would cost fifty to haul it out of here. It's the house you ought to sell."

"The house?" she said. Yes, that had been in her mind. "I'd have to get twenty thousand for it."

"Eight is a fair price."

"Fifteen. . . ." She was offended, and her voice recovered its strength. "India put eight into it in two years. And don't forget that Sego Lake is one of the most beautiful places in the world."

"But where is it? Five hundred and some miles to San Francisco and two hundred to Salt Lake City. Who wants to live way out here but a few eccentrics like you and India? And me?"

"There are things you can't put a price tag on. Beautiful things."

"Oh, bull, Hattie! You don't know squat about beautiful things. Any more than I do. I live here because it figures for me, and you because India left you the house. And just in the nick of time, too. Without it you wouldn't have had a pot of your own."

His words offended Hattie; more than that, they frightened her. She was silent and then grew thoughtful, for she was fond of Jerry Rolfe and he of her. He had good sense and moreover he only expressed her own thoughts. He spoke no more than the truth about India's death and the house. But she told herself, He doesn't know everything. You'd have to pay a San Francisco architect ten thousand just to *think* of such a house. Before he drew a line.

"Jerry," the old woman said, "what am I going to do about replacing the blood in the blood bank?"

"Do you want a quart from me, Hat?" His eye began to fall shut.

"You won't do. You had that tumor, two years ago. I think Darly ought to give some."

"The old man?" Rolfe laughed at her. "You want to kill him?"

"Why!" said Hattie with anger, lifting up her massive face. Fever and perspiration had frayed the fringe of curls; at the back of the head the hair had knotted and matted so that it had to be shaved. "Darly almost killed me. It's his fault that I'm in this condition. He must have *some* blood in him. He runs after all the chicks—all of them—young and old."

"Come, you were drunk, too," said Rolfe.

"I've driven drunk for forty years. It was the sneeze. Oh, Jerry, I feel wrung out," said Hattie, haggard, sitting forward in bed. But her face was cleft by her nonsensically happy grin. She was not one to be miserable for long; she had the expression of a perennial survivor.

Every other day she went to the therapist. The young woman worked her arm for her; it was a pleasure and a comfort to Hattie, who would have been glad to leave the whole cure to her. However, she was given other exercises to do, and these were not so easy. They rigged a pulley for her and Hattie had to hold both ends of a rope and saw it back and forth through the scraping little wheel. She bent heavily from the hips and coughed over her cigarette. But the most important exercise of all she shirked. This required her to put the flat of her hand to the wall at the level of her hips and, by working her finger tips slowly, to make the hand ascend to the height of her shoulder. That was painful; she often forgot to do it, although the doctor warned her, "Hattie, you don't want adhesions, do you?"

A light of despair crossed Hattie's eyes. Then she said, "Oh, Dr. Stroud, buy my house from me."

"I'm a bachelor. What would I do with a house?"

"I know just the girl for you—my cousin's daughter. Perfectly charming and very brainy. Just about got her Ph.D."

"You must get quite a few proposals yourself," said the doctor.

"From crazy desert rats. They chase me. But," she said, "after I pay my bills I'll be in pretty punk shape. If at least I could replace that blood in the blood bank I'd feel easier."

"If you don't do as the therapist tells you, Hattie, you'll need another operation. Do you know what adhesions are?"

She knew. But Hattie thought, *How long must I go on taking care of myself?* It made her angry to hear him speak of another operation. She had a moment of panic, but she covered it up. With him, this young man whose skin was already as thick as buttermilk and whose chestnut hair was as dry as death, she always assumed the part of a child. In a small voice she said, "Yes, doctor." But her heart was in a fury.

Night and day, however, she repeated, "I was in the Valley of the Shadow. But I'm alive." She was weak, she was old, she couldn't follow a train of thought very easily, she felt faint in the head. But she was still here; here was her body, it filled space, a great body. And though she had worries and perplexities, and once in a while her arm felt as though it was about to give her the last stab of all; and though her hair was scrappy and old, like onion roots, and scattered like nothing under the comb, yet she sat and amused herself with visitors; her great grin split her face; her heart warmed with every kind word.

And she thought, People will help me out. It never did me any good to worry. At the last minute something turned up, when I wasn't looking for it. Marian loves me. Helen and Jerry love me. Half Pint loves me. They would never let me go to the ground. And I love them. If it were the other way around, I'd never let them go down.

Above the horizon, in a baggy vastness which Hattie by herself occasionally visited, the features of India, her *shade*, sometimes rose. India was indignant and scolding. Not mean. Not really mean. Few people had ever been really mean to Hattie. But India was annoyed with her. "The garden is going to hell, Hattie," she said. "Those lilac bushes are all shriveled."

"But what can I do? The hose is rotten. It broke. It won't reach."

"Then dig a trench," said the phantom of India. "Have old Sam dig a trench. But save the bushes."

Am I thy servant still? said Hattie to herself. *No*, she thought, *let the dead bury their dead.*

But she didn't defy India now any more than she had done when they lived together. Hattie was supposed to keep India off the bottle, but often both of them began to get drunk after breakfast. They forgot to dress, and in their slips the two of them wandered drunkenly around the house and blundered into each other, and they were in despair at having been so weak. Late in the afternoon they would be sitting in the living room, waiting for the sun to set. It shrank, burning itself out on the crumbling edges of the mountains. When the sun passed, the fury of the daylight ended and the mountain surfaces were more blue, broken, like cliffs of coal. They no longer suggested faces. The east began to look simple, and the lake less inhuman and haughty. At last India would say, "Hattie—it's time for the lights." And Hattie would pull the switch chains of the lamps, several of them, to give the generator a good shove. She would turn on some of the wobbling eighteenth-century-style lamps whose shades stood out from their slender bodies like dragonflies' wings. The little engine in the shed would shuffle, then spit, then charge and bang, and the first weak light would rise unevenly in the bulbs.

"Hettie!" cried India. After she drank she was penitent, but her penitence too was a hardship to Hattie, and the worse her temper the more British her accent became. *"Where the hell ah you Het-tie!"* After India's death Hattie found some poems she had written in which she, Hattie, was affectionately and even touchingly mentioned. That was a good thing—Literature. Education. Breeding. But Hattie's interest in ideas was very small, whereas India had been all over the world. India was used to brilliant society. India wanted her to discuss Eastern religion, Bergson and Proust, and Hattie had no head for this, and so India blamed her drinking on Hattie. "I can't talk to you," she would say. "You don't understand religion or culture. And I'm here because I'm not fit to be anywhere else. I can't live in New York any more. It's too dangerous for a woman my age to be drunk in the street at night."

And Hattie, talking to her Western friends about India, would say, "She is a lady" (implying that they made a pair). "She is a creative person" (this was why they found each other so congenial). "But helpless? Completely. Why she can't even get her own girdle on."

"Hettie! Come here. Het-tie! Do you know what sloth is?"

Undressed, India sat on her bed and with the cigarette in her drunken, wrinkled, ringed hand she burned holes in the blankets. On Hattie's pride she left many small scars, too. She treated her like a servant.

Weeping, India begged Hattie afterward to forgive her. *"Hattie, please don't condemn me in your heart. Forgive me, dear, I know I am bad. But I hurt myself more in my evil than I hurt you."*

Hattie would keep a stiff bearing. She would lift up her face with its incurved nose and puffy eyes and say, "I am a Christian person. I never bear a grudge." And by repeating this she actually brought herself to forgive India.

But of course Hattie had no husband, no child, no skill, no savings. And what she would have done if India had not died and left her the yellow house nobody knows.

Jerry Rolfe said privately to Marian, "Hattie can't do anything for herself. If I hadn't been around during the forty-four blizzard she and India both would have starved. She's always been careless and lazy and now she can't even chase a cow out of the yard. She's too feeble. The thing for her to do is to go East to her damn brother. Hattie would have ended at the poor farm if it hadn't been for India. But besides the damn house India should have left her some dough. She didn't use her goddamn head."

When Hattie returned to the lake she stayed with the Rolfes. "Well, old shellback," said Jerry, "there's a little more life in you now."

Indeed, with joyous eyes, the cigarette in her mouth and her hair newly frizzed and overhanging her forehead, she seemed to have triumphed again. She was pale, but she grinned, she chuckled, and she held a bourbon old-fashioned with a cherry and a slice of orange in it. She was on rations; the Rolfes allowed her two a day. Her back, Helen noted, was more bent than before. Her knees went outward a little weakly; her feet, however, came close together at the ankles.

"Oh, Helen dear and Jerry dear, I am so thankful, so glad to be back at the lake. I can look after my place again, and I'm here to see the spring. It's more gorgeous than ever."

Heavy rains had fallen while Hattie was away. The sego lilies, which bloomed only after a wet winter, came up from the loose dust, especially around the marl pit; but even on the burnt granite they seemed to grow. Desert peach was beginning to appear, and in Hattie's yard the rosebushes were filling out. The roses were yellow and abundant, and the odor they gave off was like that of damp tea leaves.

"Before it gets hot enough for the rattlesnakes," said Hattie to Helen, "we ought to drive up to Marky's ranch and gather watercress."

Hattie was going to attend to lots of things, but the heat came early that year and, as there was no television to keep her awake, she slept most of the day. She was now able to dress herself, though there was little more that she could do. Sam Jervis rigged the pulley for her on the porch and she remembered once in a while to use it. Mornings when she had her strength she rambled over to her own house, examining things, being important and giving orders to Sam Jervis and Wanda Gingham. At ninety, Wanda, a Shoshone, was still an excellent seamstress and housecleaner.

Hattie looked over the car, which was parked under a cottonwood tree. She tested the engine. Yes, the old pot would still go. Proudly, happily, she listened to the noise of tappets; the dry old pipe shook as the smoke went out at the rear. She tried to work the shift, turn the wheel. That, as yet, she couldn't do. But it would come soon, she was confident.

At the back of the house the soil had caved in a little over the cesspool and a few of the old railroad ties over the top had rotted. Otherwise things were in good shape. Sam had looked after the garden. He had fixed a new catch for the gate after Pace's horses—maybe because he could never afford to keep them in hay—had broken in and Sam found them grazing and drove them out. Luckily, they hadn't damaged many of her plants. Hattie felt a moment of wild rage against Pace. He had brought the horses into her garden for a free feed, she was sure. But her anger didn't last long. It was reabsorbed into the feeling of golden pleasure that enveloped her. She had little strength, but all that she had was a pleasure to her. So she forgave even Pace, who would have liked to do her out of the house, who had always used her, embarrassed her, cheated her at cards, swindled her. All that he did he did for the sake of his quarter horses. He was a fool about horses. They were ruining him. Racing horses was a millionaire's amusement.

She saw his animals in the distance, feeding. Unsaddled, the mares appeared undressed; they reminded her of naked women walking with their glossy flanks in the sego lilies which curled on the ground. The flowers were yellowish, like winter wool, but fragrant; the mares, naked and gentle, walked through them. Their strolling, their perfect beauty, the sound of their hoofs on stone touched a deep place in Hattie's nature. Her love for horses, birds, and dogs was well known. Dogs led the list. And now a piece cut from a green blanket reminded Hattie of her dog Richie. The blanket was one he had torn, and she had cut it into strips and placed them under the doors to keep out the drafts. In the house she found more traces of him: hair he had shed on the furniture. Hattie was going to borrow Helen's vacuum cleaner, but there wasn't really enough current to make it pull as it should. On the doorknob of India's room hung the dog collar.

Hattie had decided that she would have herself moved into India's bed when it was time to die. Why should there be two deathbeds? A perilous look came into her eyes, her lips were pressed together forbiddingly. *I follow,* she said, speaking to India with an inner voice, *so never mind.* Presently—before long—she would have to leave the yellow house in her turn. And as she went into the parlor, thinking of the will, she sighed. Pretty soon she would have to attend to it. India's lawyer, Claiborne, helped her with such things.

She had phoned him in town, while she was staying with Marian, and talked matters over with him. He had promised to try to sell the house for her. Fifteen thousand was her bottom price, she said. If he couldn't find a buyer, perhaps he could find a tenant. Two hundred dollars a month was the rental she set. Rolfe laughed. Hattie turned toward him one of those proud, dulled looks she always took on when he angered her. Haughtily she said, "For summer on Sego Lake? That's reasonable."

"You're competing with Pace's ranch."

"Why, the food is stinking down there. And he cheats the dudes," said Hattie. "He really cheats them at cards. You'll never catch me playing blackjack with him again."

And what would she do, thought Hattie, if Claiborne could neither rent nor sell the house? This question she shook off as regularly as it returned. *I don't have to be a burden on anybody,* thought Hattie. *It's looked bad many a time before, but when push came to shove, I made it. Somehow I got by.* But she argued with herself: *How many times? How long, O God—an old thing, feeble, no use to anyone?* Who said she had any right to own property?

She was sitting on her sofa, which was very old—India's sofa—eight feet long, kidney-shaped, puffy, and bald. An underlying pink shone through the green; the upholstered tufts were like the pads of dogs' paws; between them rose bunches of hair. Here Hattie slouched, resting, with knees wide apart and a cigarette in her mouth, eyes half-shut but farseeing. The mountains seemed not fifteen miles but fifteen hundred feet away, the lake a blue band; the tealike odor of the roses, though they were still unopened, was already in the air, for Sam was watering them in the heat. Gratefully Hattie yelled, "Sam!"

Sam was very old, and all shanks. His feet looked big. His old railroad jacket was made tight across the back by his stoop. A crooked finger with its great broad nail over the mouth of the hose made the water spray and sparkle.

Happy to see Hattie, he turned his long jaw, empty of teeth, and his long blue eyes, which seemed to bend back to penetrate into his temples (it was his face that turned, not his body), and he said, "Oh, there, Hattie. You've made it home today? Welcome, Hattie."

"Have a beer, Sam. Come around the kitchen door and I'll give you a beer."

She never had Sam in the house, owing to his skin disease. There were raw patches on his chin and behind his ears. Hattie feared infection from his touch, having decided that he had impetigo. She gave him the beer can, never a glass, and she put on gloves before she used the garden tools. Since he would take no money from her—Wanda Gingham charged a dollar a day—she got Marian to find old clothes for him in town and she left food for him at the door of the damp-wood-smelling boxcar where he lived.

"How's the old wing, Hat?" he said.

"It's coming. I'll be driving the car again before you know it," she told him. "By the first of May I'll be driving again." Every week she moved the date forward. "By Decoration Day I expect to be on my own again," she said.

In mid-June, however, she was still unable to drive. Helen Rolfe said to her, "Hattie, Jerry and I are due in Seattle the first week of July."

"Why, you never told me that," said Hattie.

"You don't mean to tell me this is the first you heard of it," said Helen. "You've known about it from the first—since Christmas."

It wasn't easy for Hattie to meet her eyes. She presently put her head down. Her face became very dry, especially the lips. "Well, don't you worry about me. I'll be all right here," she said.

"Who's going to look after you?" said Jerry. He evaded nothing himself and tolerated no evasion in others. Except that, as Hattie knew, he made every possible allowance for her. But who would help her? She couldn't count on her friend Half Pint, she couldn't really count on Marian either. She had had only the Rolfes to turn to. Helen, trying to be steady, gazed at her and made sad, involuntary movements with her head, sometimes nodding, sometimes seeming as if she disagreed. Hattie, with her inner voice, swore at her: *Bitch-eyes. I can't make it the way she does because I'm old. Is that fair?* And yet she admired Helen's eyes. Even the skin about them, slightly wrinkled, heavy underneath, was touching, beautiful. There was a heaviness in her bust that went, as if by attachment, with the heaviness of her eyes. Her head, her hands and feet should have taken a more slender body. Helen, said Hattie, was the nearest thing she had on earth to a sister. But there was no reason to go to Seattle—no genuine business. Why the hell Seattle? It was only idleness, only a holiday. The only reason was Hattie herself; this was their way of telling her that there was a limit to what she could expect them to do for her. Helen's nervous head wavered, but her thoughts were steady. She knew what was passing through Hattie's mind. Like Hattie, she was an idle woman. Why was her right to idleness better?

Because of money? thought Hattie. Because of age? Because she has a husband? Because she had a daughter in Swarthmore College? But an interesting thing occurred to her. Helen disliked being idle, whereas Hattie herself had never made any bones about it: an idle life was all she was good for. But for her it had been uphill all the way, because when Waggoner divorced her she didn't have a cent. She even had to support Wicks for seven or eight years. Except with horses, Wicks had no sense. And then she had had to take tons of dirt from India. *I am the one*, Hattie asserted to herself. *I would know what to do with Helen's advantages. She only suffers from them. And if she wants to stop being an idle woman why can't she start with me, her neighbor?* Hattie's skin, for all its puffiness, burned with anger. She said to Rolfe and Helen, "Don't worry. I'll make out. But if I have to leave the lake you'll be ten times more lonely than before. Now I'm going back to my house."

She lifted up her broad old face, and her lips were child-like with suffering. She would never take back what she had said.

But the trouble was no ordinary trouble. Hattie was herself aware that she rambled, forgot names, and answered when no one spoke.

"We can't just take charge of her," Rolfe said. "What's more, she ought to be near a doctor. She keeps her shotgun loaded so she can fire it if anything happens to her in the house. But who knows what she'll shoot? I don't believe it was Jacamares who killed that Doberman of hers."

Rolfe drove into the yard the day after she moved back to the yellow house and said, "I'm going into town. I can bring you some chow if you like."

She couldn't afford to refuse his offer, angry though she was, and she said, "Yes, bring me some stuff from the Mountain Street Market. Charge it." She had only some frozen shrimp and a few cans of beer in the icebox. When Rolfe had gone she put out the package of shrimp to thaw.

People really used to stick by one another in the West. Hattie now saw herself as one of the pioneers. The modern breed had come later. After all, she had lived on the range like an old-timer. Wicks had had to shoot their Christmas dinner and she had cooked it——venison. He killed it on the reservation, and if the Indians had caught them, there would have been hell to pay.

The weather was hot, the clouds were heavy and calm in a large sky. The horizon was so huge that in it the lake must have seemed like a saucer of milk. *Some milk!* Hattie thought. Two thousand feet down in the middle, so deep no corpse could ever be recovered. A body, they said, went around with the currents. And there were rocks like eye-teeth, and hot springs, and colorless fish at the bottom which were never caught. Now that the white pelicans

were nesting they patrolled the rocks for snakes and other
egg thieves. They were so big and flew so slow you might
imagine they were angels. Hattie no longer visited the lake
shore; the walk exhausted her. She saved her strength to go
to Pace's bar in the afternoon.

She took off her shoes and stockings and walked on bare
feet from one end of her house to the other. On the land
side she saw Wanda Gingham sitting near the tracks while
her great-grandson played in the soft red gravel. Wanda
wore a large purple shawl and her black head was bare. All
about her was—was nothing, Hattie thought; for she had
taken a drink, breaking her rule. Nothing but mountains,
thrust out like men's bodies; the sagebrush was the hair on
their chests.

The warm wind blew dust from the marl pit. This white
powder made her sky less blue. On the water side were the
pelicans, pure as spirits, slow as angels, blessing the air as
they flew with great wings.

Should she or should she not have Sam do something
about the vine on the chimney? Sparrows nested in it, and
she was glad of that. But all summer long the king snakes
were after them and she was afraid to walk in the garden.
When the sparrows scratched the ground for seed they took
a funny bound; they held their legs stiff and flung back the
dust with both feet. Hattie sat down at her old Spanish
monastery table, watching them in the cloudy warmth of
the day, clasping her hands, chuckling and sad. The bushes
were crowded with yellow roses, half of them now rotted.
The lizards scrambled from shadow to shadow. The water
was smooth as air, gaudy as silk. The mountains suc-
cumbed, falling asleep in the heat. Drowsy, Hattie lay
down on her sofa, its pads to her always like dogs' paws.
She gave in to sleep and when she woke it was midnight;
she did not want to alarm the Rolfes by putting on her
lights so she took advantage of the moon to eat a few
thawed shrimps and go to the bathroom. She undressed

and lifted herself into bed and lay there feeling her sore arm. Now she knew how much she missed her dog. The whole matter of the dog weighed heavily on her soul. She came close to tears, thinking about him, and she went to sleep oppressed by her secret.

I suppose I had better try to pull myself together a little, thought Hattie nervously in the morning. *I can't just sleep my way through.* She knew what her difficulty was. Before any serious question her mind gave way. It scattered or diffused. She said to herself, *I can see bright, but I feel dim. I guess I'm not so lively any more. Maybe I'm becoming a little touched in the head, as Mother was.* But she was not so old as her mother was when she did those strange things. At eighty-five, her mother had to be kept from going naked in the street. *I'm not as bad as that yet. Thank God! Yes, I walked into the men's wards, but that was when I had a fever, and my nightie was on.*

She drank a cup of Nescafé and it strengthened her determination to do something for herself. In all the world she had only her brother Angus to go to. Her brother Will had led a rough life; he was an old heller, and now he drove everyone away. He was too crabby, thought Hattie. Besides he was angry because she had lived so long with Wicks. Angus would forgive her. But then he and his wife were not her kind. With them she couldn't drink, she couldn't smoke, she had to make herself small-mouthed, and she would have to wait while they read a chapter of the Bible before breakfast. Hattie could not bear to sit at table waiting for meals. Besides, she had a house of her own at last. Why should she have to leave it? She had never owned a thing before. And now she was not allowed to enjoy her yellow house. *But I'll keep it,* she said to herself rebelliously. *I swear to God I'll keep it. Why, I barely just got it. I haven't had time.* And she went out on the porch to work the pulley and do something about the adhesions in her arm. She was sure now that they were there. *And.*

what will I do? she cried to herself. *What will I do? Why did I ever go to Rolfe's that night—and why did I lose control on the crossing?* She couldn't say, now, "I sneezed." She couldn't even remember what had happened, except that she saw the boulders and the twisting blue rails and Darly. It was Darly's fault. He was sick and old himself. *He* couldn't make it. He envied her the house, and her woman's peaceful life. Since she returned from the hospital he hadn't even come to visit her. He only said, "Hell, I'm sorry for her, but it was her fault." What hurt him most was that she had said he couldn't hold his liquor.

Fierceness, swearing to God did no good. She was still the same procrastinating old woman. She had a letter to answer from Hotchkiss Insurance and it drifted out of sight. She was going to phone Claiborne the lawyer, but it slipped her mind. One morning she announced to Helen that she believed she would apply to an institution in Los Angeles that took over the property of old people and managed it for them. They gave you an apartment right on the ocean, and your meals and medical care. You had to sign over half of your estate. "It's fair enough," said Hattie. "They take a gamble. I may live to be a hundred."

"I wouldn't be surprised," said Helen.

However, Hattie never got around to sending to Los Angeles for the brochure. But Jerry Rolfe took it on himself to write a letter to her brother Angus about her condition. And he drove over also to have a talk with Amy Walters, the gold miner's widow at Fort Walters—as the ancient woman called it. The Fort was an old tar-paper building over the mine. The shaft made a cesspool unnecessary. Since the death of her second husband no one had dug for gold. On a heap of stones near the road a crimson sign FORT WALTERS was placed. Behind it was a flagpole. The American flag was raised every day.

Amy was working in the garden in one of dead Bill's

shirts. Bill had brought water down from the mountains for her in a homemade aqueduct so she could raise her own peaches and vegetables.

"Amy," Rolfe said, "Hattie's back from the hospital and living all alone. You have no folks and neither has she. Not to beat around the bush about it, why don't you live together?"

Amy's face had great delicacy. Her winter baths in the lake, her vegetable soups, the waltzes she played for herself alone on the grand piano that stood beside her wood stove, the murder stories she read till darkness obliged her to close the book—this life of hers had made her remote. She looked delicate, yet there was no way to affect her composure, she couldn't be touched. It was very strange.

"Hattie and me have different habits, Jerry," said Amy. "And Hattie wouldn't like my company. I can't drink with her. I'm a teetotaller."

"That's true," said Rolfe, recalling that Hattie referred to Amy as if she were a ghost. He couldn't speak to Amy of the solitary death in store for her. There was not a cloud in the arid sky today, and there was no shadow of death on Amy. She was tranquil, she seemed to be supplied with a sort of pure fluid that would feed her life slowly for years to come.

He said, "All kinds of things could happen to a woman like Hattie in that yellow house, and nobody would know."

"That's a fact. She doesn't know how to take care of herself."

"She can't. Her arm hasn't healed."

Amy didn't say that she was sorry to hear it. In the place of those words came a silence which might have meant that. Then she said, "I might go over there a few hours a day, but she would have to pay me."

"Now, Amy, you must know as well as I do that Hattie has no money—not much more than her pension. Just the house."

At once Amy said, no pause coming between his words and hers, "I would take care of her if she'd agree to leave the house to me."

"Leave it in your hands, you mean?" said Rolfe. "To manage?"

"In her will. To belong to me."

"Why, Amy, what would you do with Hattie's house?" he said.

"It would be my property, that's all. I'd have it."

"Maybe you would leave Fort Walters to her in your will," he said.

"Oh, no," she said. "Why should I? I'm not asking Hattie for her help. I don't need it. Hattie is a city woman."

Rolfe could not carry this proposal back to Hattie. He was too wise ever to mention her will to her.

But Pace was not so careful of her feelings. By mid-June Hattie had begun to visit his bar regularly. She had so many things to think about she couldn't stay at home. When Pace came in from the yard one day—he had been packing the wheels of his horse-trailer and was wiping grease from his fingers—he said with his usual bluntness, "How would you like it if I paid you fifty bucks a month for the rest of your life, Hat?"

Hattie was holding her second old-fashioned of the day. At the bar she made it appear that she observed the limit; but she had started drinking at home. One before lunch, one during, one after lunch. She began to grin, expecting Pace to make one of his jokes. But he was wearing his scoop-shaped Western hat as level as a Quaker, and he had drawn down his chin, a sign that he was not fooling. She said, "That would be nice, but what's the catch?"

"No catch," he said. "This is what we'd do. I'd give you five hundred dollars cash, and fifty bucks a month for life, and you let me sleep some dudes in the yellow house, and you'd leave the house to me in your will."

"What kind of a deal is that?" said Hattie, her look changing. "I thought we were friends."

"It's the best deal you'll ever get," he said.

The weather was sultry, but Hattie till now had thought that it was nice. She had been dreamy but comfortable, about to begin to enjoy the cool of the day; but now she felt that such cruelty and injustice had been waiting to attack her, that it would have been better to die in the hospital than be so disillusioned.

She cried, "Everybody wants to push me out. You're a cheater, Pace. God! I know you. Pick on somebody else. Why do you have to pick on me? Just because I happen to be around?"

"Why, no, Hattie," he said, trying now to be careful. "It was just a business offer."

"Why don't you give me some blood for the bank if you're such a friend of mine?"

"Well, Hattie, you drink too much and you oughtn't to have been driving anyway."

"I sneezed, and you know it. The whole thing happened because I sneezed. Everybody knows that. I wouldn't sell you my house. I'd give it away to the lepers first. You'd let me go away and never send me a cent. You never pay anybody. You can't even buy wholesale in town any more because nobody trusts you. I'm stuck, that's all, just stuck. I keep on saying that this is my only home in all the world, this is where my friends are, and the weather is always perfect and the lake is beautiful. But I wish the whole damn empty old place were in Hell. It's not human and neither are you. But I'll be here the day the sheriff takes away your horses—you never mind! I'll be clapping and applauding!"

He told her then that she was drunk again, and so she was, but she was more than that, and though her head was spinning she decided to go back to the house at once and take care of some things she had been putting off. This very day she was going to write to the lawyer, Claiborne, and make sure that Pace never got her property. She wouldn't put it past him to swear in court that India had promised him the yellow house.

She sat at the table with pen and paper, trying to think how to put it.

"I want this on record," she wrote. "I could kick myself in the head when I think of how he's led me on. I have been his patsy ten thousand times. As when that drunk crashed his Cub plane on the lake shore. At the coroner's jury he let me take the whole blame. He said he had instructed me when I was working for him never to take in any drunks. And this flier was drunk. He had nothing on but a T shirt and Bermuda shorts and he was flying from Sacramento to Salt Lake City. At the inquest Pace said I had disobeyed his instructions. The same was true when the cook went haywire. She was a tramp. He never hires decent help. He cheated her on the bar bill and blamed me and she went after me with a meat cleaver. She disliked me because I criticized her for drinking at the bar in her one-piece white bathing suit with the dude guests. But he turned her loose on me. He hints that he did certain services for India. She would never have let him touch one single finger. He was too common for her. It can never be said about India that she was not a lady in every way. He thinks he is the greatest sack-artist in the world. He only loves horses, as a fact. He has no claims at all, oral or written, on this yellow house. I want you to have this over my signature. He was cruel to Pickle-Tits who was his first wife, and he's no better to the charming woman who is his present one. I don't know why she takes it. It must be despair." Hattie said to herself, *I don't suppose I'd better send that.*

She was still angry. Her heart was knocking within; the deep pulses, as after a hot bath, beat at the back of her thighs. The air outside was dotted with transparent particles. The mountains were as red as furnace clinkers. The iris leaves were fan sticks—they stuck out like Jiggs's hair.

She always ended by looking out of the window at the desert and lake. *They drew you from yourself. But after they had drawn you, what did they do with you? It was too late to find out. I'll never know. I wasn't meant to. I'm not the type,* Hattie reflected. *Maybe something too cruel for women, young or old.*

So she stood up and, rising, she had the sensation that she had gradually become a container for herself. You get old, your heart, your liver, your lungs seem to expand in size, and the walls of the body give way outward, swelling, she thought, and you take the shape of an old jug, wider and wider toward the top. You swell up with tears and fat. She no longer even smelled to herself like a woman. Her face with its much-slept-upon skin was only faintly like her own—like a cloud that has changed. It was a face. It became a ball of yarn. It had drifted open. It had scattered.

I was never one single thing anyway, she thought. *Never my own. I was only loaned to myself.*

But the thing wasn't over yet. And in fact she didn't know for certain that it was ever going to be over. You only had other people's word for it that death was such-and-such. How do I know? she asked herself challengingly. Her anger had sobered her for a little while. Now she was again drunk. . . . *It was strange. It is strange. It may continue being strange.* She further thought, *I used to wish for death more than I do now. Because I didn't have anything at all. I changed when I got a roof of my own over me. And now? Do I have to go? I thought Marian loved me, but she already has a sister. And I thought Helen and Jerry would never desert me, but they've beat it. And now Pace has insulted me. They think I'm not going to make it.*

She went to the cupboard—she kept the bourbon bottle there; she drank less if each time she had to rise and open the cupboard door. And, as if she were being watched, she poured a drink and swallowed it.

The notion that in this emptiness someone saw her was connected with the other notion that she was being filmed from birth to death. That this was done for everyone. And afterward you could view your life. A hereafter movie.

Hattie wanted to see some of it now, and she sat down on the dogs'-paw cushions of her sofa and, with her knees far apart and a smile of yearning and of fright, she bent her round back, burned a cigarette at the corner of her mouth and saw—the Church of Saint Sulpice in Paris where her organ teacher used to bring her. It looked like country walls of stone, but rising high and leaning outward were towers. She was very young. She knew music. How she could ever have been so clever was beyond her. But she did know it. She could read all those notes. The sky was gray. After this she saw some entertaining things she liked to tell people about. She was a young wife. She was in Aix-les-Bains with her mother-in-law, and they played bridge in a mud bath with a British general and his aide. There were artificial waves in the swimming pool. She lost her bathing suit because it was a size too big. How did she get out? Ah, you got out of everything.

She saw her husband, James John Waggoner IV. They were snow-bound together in New Hampshire. "Jimmy, Jimmy, how can you fling a wife away?" she asked him. "Have you forgotten love? Did I drink too much—did I bore you?" He had married again and had two children. He had gotten tired of her. And though he was a vain man with nothing to be vain about—no looks, not too much intelligence, nothing but an old Philadelphia family—she had loved him. She too had been a snob about her Philadelphia connections. Give up the name of Waggoner? How could she? For this reason she had never married Wicks. "How dare you," she had said to Wicks, "come without a shave in a dirty shirt and muck on you, come and ask me to marry!

If you want to propose, go and clean up first." But his dirt was only a pretext.

Trade Waggoner for Wicks? she asked herself again with a swing of her shoulders. She wouldn't think of it. Wicks was an excellent man. But he was a cowboy. Socially nothing. He couldn't even read. But she saw this on her film. They were in Athens Canyon, in a cratelike house, and she was reading aloud to him from *The Count of Monte Cristo*. He wouldn't let her stop. While walking to stretch her legs, she read, and he followed her about to catch each word. After all, he was very dear to her. Such a man! Now she saw him jump from his horse. They were living on the range, trapping coyotes. It was just the second gray of evening, cloudy, moments after the sun had gone down. There was an animal in the trap, and he went toward it to kill it. He wouldn't waste a bullet on the creatures but killed them with a kick, with his boot. And then Hattie saw that this coyote was all white—snarling teeth, white scruff. "Wicks, he's white! White as a polar bear. You're not going to kill him, are you?" The animal flattened to the ground. He snarled and cried. He couldn't pull away because of the heavy trap. And Wicks killed him. What else could he have done? The white beast lay dead. The dust of Wicks's boots hardly showed on its head and jaws. Blood ran from the muzzle.

And now came something on Hattie's film she tried to shun. It was she herself who had killed her dog, Richie. Just as Rolfe and Pace had warned her, he was vicious, his brain was turned. She, because she was on the side of all dumb creatures, defended him when he bit the trashy woman Jacamares was living with. Perhaps if she had had Richie from a puppy he wouldn't have turned on her. When she got him he was already a year and a half old and she couldn't break him of his habits. But she thought that only she understood him. And Rolfe had warned her, "You'll be

sued, do you know that? The dog will take out after somebody smarter than that Jacamares's woman, and you'll be
in for it."

Hattie saw herself as she swayed her shoulders and said,
"Nonsense."

But what fear she had felt when the dog went for her on
the porch. Suddenly she could see, by his skull, by his eyes
that he was evil. She screamed at him, "Richie!" And what
had she done to him? He had lain under the gas range all
day growling and wouldn't come out. She tried to urge him
out with the broom, and he snatched it in his teeth. She
pulled him out, and he left the stick and tore at her. Now,
as the spectator of this, her eyes opened, beyond the preg-
nant curtain and the air-wave of marl dust, summer's
snow, drifting over the water. "Oh, my God! Richie!" Her
thigh was snatched by his jaws. His teeth went through her
skirt. She felt she would fall. Would she go down? Then
the dog would rush at her throat—then black night, bad-
odored mouth, the blood pouring from her neck, from torn
veins. Her heart shriveled as the teeth went into her thigh,
and she couldn't delay another second but took her kindling hatchet from the nail, strengthened her grip on the
smooth wood, and hit the dog. She saw the blow. She saw
him die at once. And then in fear and shame she hid the
body. And at night she buried him in the yard. Next day
she accused Jacamares. On him she laid the blame for the
disappearance of her dog.

She stood up; she spoke to herself in silence, as was her
habit. *God, what shall I do? I have taken life. I have lied. I
have borne false witness. I have stalled. And now what
shall I do? Nobody will help me.*

And suddenly she made up her mind that she should go
and do what she had been putting off for weeks, namely,
test herself with the car, and she slipped on her shoes and
went outside. Lizards ran before her in the thirsty dust. She
opened the hot, broad door of the car. She lifted her lame

hand onto the wheel. With her right hand she reached far
to the left and turned the wheel with all her might. Then
she started the motor and tried to drive out of the yard. But
she could not release the emergency brake with its rasplike
rod. She reached with her good hand, the right, under the
steering wheel and pressed her bosom on it and strained.
No, she could not shift the gears and steer. She couldn't
even reach down to the hand brake. The sweat broke out on
her skin. Her efforts were too much. She was deeply
wounded by the pain in her arm. The door of the car fell
open again and she turned from the wheel and with her
stiff legs hanging from the door she wept. What could she
do now? And when she had wept over the ruin of her life
she got out of the old car and went back to the house. She
took the bourbon from the cupboard and picked up the ink
bottle and a pad of paper and sat down to write her will.

"My Will," she wrote, and sobbed to herself.

Since the death of India she had numberless times asked
the question, To Whom? Who will get this when I die? She
had unconsciously put people to the test to find out whether
they were worthy. It made her more severe than before.

Now she wrote, "I Harriet Simmons Waggoner, being of
sound mind and not knowing what may be in store for me
at the age of seventy-two (born 1885), living alone at Sego
Desert Lake, instruct my lawyer, Harold Claiborne, Paiute
County Court Building, to draw my last will and testament
upon the following terms."

She sat perfectly still now to hear from within who
would be the lucky one, who would inherit the yellow
house. For which she had waited. Yes, waited for India's
death, choking on her bread because she was a rich
woman's servant and whipping girl. But who had done for
her, Hattie, what she had done for India? And who, apart
from India, had ever held out a hand to her? Kindness, yes.
Here and there people had been kind. But the word in her
head was not kindness, it was succor. And who had given

her that? *Succor?* Only India. If at least, next best after succor, someone had given her a shake and said, "Stop stalling.
Don't be such a slow, old, procrastinating sit-stiller." Again,
it was only India who had done her good. She had offered
her succor. "Het-tie!" said that drunken mask. "Do you
know what sloth is? Demn you! poky old demned thing!"

But I was waiting, Hattie realized. *I was waiting, thinking, "Youth is terrible, frightening. I will wait it out. And
men? Men are cruel and strong. They want things I haven't
got to give." There were no kids in me,* thought Hattie. *Not
that I wouldn't have loved them, but such my nature was.
And who can blame me for having it? My nature?*

She drank from an old-fashioned glass. There was no
orange in it, no ice, no bitters or sugar, only the stinging,
clear bourbon.

So then, she continued, looking at the dry sun-stamped
dust and the last freckled flowers of red wild peach, *to live
with Angus and his wife? And to have to hear a chapter
from the Bible before breakfast? Once more in the house—
not of a stranger, perhaps, but not far from it either?* In
other houses, in someone else's house, to wait for meal-
times was her lifelong punishment. She always felt it in the
throat and stomach. And so she would again, and to the
very end. However, she must think of someone to leave the
house to.

And first of all she wanted to do right by her family.
None of them had ever dreamed that she, Hattie, would
ever have something to bequeath. Until a few years ago it
had certainly looked as if she would die a pauper. So now
she could keep her head up with the proudest of them. And,
as this occurred to her, she actually lifted up her face with
its broad nose and victorious eyes; if her hair had become
shabby as onion roots, if, at the back, her head was round
and bald as a newel post, what did that matter? Her heart
experienced a childish glory, not yet tired of it after seventy-
two years. She, too, had amounted to something. *I'll do*

some good by going, she thought. *Now I believe I should leave it to, to . . .* She returned to the old point of struggle. She had decided many times and many times changed her mind. She tried to think, *Who would get the most out of this yellow house?* It was a tearing thing to go through. If it had not been the house but, instead, some brittle thing she could hold in her hand, then her last action would be to throw and smash it, and so the thing and she herself would be demolished together. But it was vain to think such thoughts. To whom should she leave it? Her brothers? Not they. Nephews? One was a submarine commander. The other was a bachelor in the State Department. Then began the roll call of cousins. Merton? He owned an estate in Connecticut. Anna? She had a face like a hot-water bottle. That left Joyce, the orphaned daughter of her cousin Wilfred. Joyce was the most likely heiress. Hattie had already written to her and had her out to the lake at Thanksgiving, two years ago. But this Joyce was another odd one; over thirty, good, yes, but placid, running to fat, a scholar —ten years in Eugene, Oregon, working for her degree. In Hattie's opinion this was only another form of sloth. Nevertheless, Joyce yet hoped to marry. Whom? Not Dr. Stroud. He wouldn't. And still Joyce had vague hopes. Hattie knew how that could be. At least have a man she could argue with.

She was now more drunk than at any time since her accident. Again she filled her glass. *Have ye eyes and see not? Sleepers awake!*

Knees wide apart she sat in the twilight, thinking. Marian? Marian didn't need another house. Half Pint? She wouldn't know what to do with it. Brother Louis came up for consideration next. He was an old actor who had a church for the Indians at Athens Canyon. Hollywood stars of the silent days sent him their negligees; he altered them and wore them in the pulpit. The Indians loved his show. But when Billy Shawah blew his brains out after his two-week bender, they still tore his shack down and turned the boards inside out to get rid of his ghost. They had their old religion. No, not Brother Louis. He'd show movies in the yellow house to the tribe or make a nursery out of it for the Indian brats.

And now she began to consider Wicks. When last heard from he was south of Bishop, California, a handy man in a saloon off toward Death Valley. It wasn't she who heard from him but Pace. Herself, she hadn't actually seen Wicks since—how low she had sunk then!—she had kept the hamburger stand on Route 158. The little lunchroom had supported them both. Wicks hung around on the end stool, rolling cigarettes (she saw it on the film). Then there was a quarrel. Things had been going from bad to worse. He'd begun to grouse now about this and now about that. He beefed about the food, at last. She saw and heard him. "Hat," he said, "I'm good and tired of hamburger." "Well, what do you think I eat?" she said with that round, defiant movement of her shoulders which she herself recognized as characteristic (*me all over*, she thought). But he opened the cash register and took out thirty cents and crossed the street to the butcher's and brought back a steak. He threw it on the griddle. "Fry it," he said. She did, and watched him eat.

And when he was through she could bear her rage no longer. "Now," she said, "you've had your meat. Get out. Never come back." She kept a pistol under the counter. She picked it up, cocked it, pointed it at his heart. "If you ever come in that door again, I'll kill you," she said.

She saw it all. *I couldn't bear to fall so low*, she thought, *to be slave to a shiftless cowboy.*

Wicks said, "Don't do that, Hat. Guess I went too far. You're right."

"You'll never have a chance to make it up," she cried. "Get out!"

On that cry he disappeared, and since then she had never seen him.

"Wicks, dear," she said. "Please! I'm sorry. Don't condemn me in your heart. Forgive me. I hurt myself in my evil. I always had a thick idiot head. I was born with a thick head."

Again she wept, for Wicks. She was too proud. A snob. Now they might have lived together in this house, old friends, simple and plain.

She thought, *He really was my good friend.*

But what would Wicks do with a house like this, alone, if he was alive and survived her? He was too wiry for soft beds or easy chairs.

And she was the one who had said stiffly to India, "I'm a Christian person. I do not bear a grudge."

Ah yes, she said to herself. *I have caught myself out too often. How long can this go on?* And she began to think, or try to think, of Joyce, her cousin's daughter. Joyce was like herself, a woman alone, getting on in years, clumsy. Probably never been laid. Too bad. She would have given much, now, to succor Joyce.

But it seemed to her now that that too, the succor, had been a story. First you heard the pure story. Then you heard the impure story. Both stories. She had paid out years, now to one shadow, now to another shadow.

Joyce would come here to the house. She had a little income and could manage. She would live as Hattie had lived, alone. Here she would rot, start to drink, maybe, and day after day read, day after day sleep. See how beautiful it was here? It burned you out. How empty! It turned you into ash.

How can I doom a younger person to the same life? asked Hattie. It's for somebody like me. When I was younger it wasn't right. But now it is, exactly. Only I fit in here. It was made for my old age, to spend my last years

peacefully. If I hadn't let Jerry make me drunk that night—
if I hadn't sneezed! Because of this arm, I'll have to live
with Angus. My heart will break there away from my only
home.

She was now very drunk, and she said to herself, *Take
what God brings. He gives no gifts unmixed. He makes
loans.*

She resumed her letter of instructions to lawyer Claiborne: "Upon the following terms," she wrote a second
time. "Because I have suffered much. Because I only lately
received what I have to give away, I can't bear it." The
drunken blood was soaring to her head. But her hand was
clear enough. She wrote, "It is too soon! Too soon! Because
I do not find it in my heart to care for anyone as I would
wish. Being cast off and lonely, and doing no harm where I
am. Why should it be? This breaks my heart. In addition to
everything else, why must I worry about this, which I must
leave? I am tormented out of my mind. Even though by my
own fault I have put myself into this position. And I am not
ready to give up on this. No, not yet. And so I'll tell you
what, I leave this property, land, house, garden, and water
rights; to Hattie Simmons Waggoner. Me! I realize this is
bad and wrong. Not possible. Yet it is the only thing I really
wish to do, so may God have mercy on my soul."

How could that happen? She studied what she had written and finally she acknowledged that she was drunk. "I'm
drunk," she said, "and don't know what I'm doing. I'll die,
and end. Like India. Dead as that lilac bush."

Then she thought that there was a beginning, and a
middle. She shrank from the last term. She began once
more—a beginning. After that, there was the early middle,
then middle middle, late middle middle, quite late middle.
In fact the middle is all I know. The rest is just a rumor.

Only tonight I can't give the house away. I'm drunk and
so I need it. And tomorrow, she promised herself, I'll think
again. I'll work it out, for sure.

THE OLD SYSTEM

It was a thoughtful day for Dr. Braun. Winter. Saturday. The short end of December. He was alone in his apartment and woke late, lying in bed until noon, in the room kept very dark, working with a thought—a feeling: Now you see it, now you don't. Now a content, now a vacancy. Now an important individual, a force, a necessary existence; suddenly nothing. A frame without a picture, a mirror with missing glass. The feeling of necessary existence might be the aggressive, instinctive vitality we share with a dog or an ape. The difference being in the power of the mind or spirit to declare *I am*. Plus the inevitable inference *I am not*. Dr. Braun was no more pleased with being than with its opposite. For him an age of equilibrium seemed to be coming in. How nice! Anyway, he had no project for putting the world in rational order, and for no special reason he got up. Washed his wrinkled but not elderly face with freezing tap water, which changed the nighttime white to a more agreeable color. He brushed his teeth. Standing upright, scrubbing the teeth as if he were looking after an idol. He then ran the big old-fashioned tub to sponge himself, backing into the thick stream of the Roman faucet, soaping beneath with the same cake of soap he would apply later to his beard. Under the swell of his belly, the tip of his parts, somewhere between his heels. His heels needed scrubbing. He dried himself with yesterday's shirt, an economy. It was going to the laundry anyway. Yes, with the self-respecting expression human beings inherit from ancestors for whom bathing was a solemnity. A sadness.

But every civilized man today cultivated an unhealthy self-detachment. Had learned from art the art of amusing self-observation and objectivity. Which, since there had to be something amusing to watch, required art in one's conduct. Existence for the sake of such practices did not seem worth while. Mankind was in a confusing, uncomfortable, disagreeable stage in the evolution of its consciousness. Dr. Braun (Samuel) did not like it. It made him sad to feel that the thought, art, belief of great traditions should be so misemployed. Elevation? Beauty? Torn into shreds, into ribbons for girls' costumes, or trailed like the tail of a kite at Happenings. Plato and the Buddha raided by looters. The tombs of Pharaohs broken into by desert rabble. And so on, thought Dr. Braun as he passed into his neat kitchen. He was well pleased by the blue-and-white Dutch dishes, cups hanging, saucers standing in slots.

He opened a fresh can of coffee, much enjoyed the fragrance from the punctured can. Only an instant, but not to be missed. Next he sliced bread for the toaster, got out the butter, chewed an orange; and he was admiring long icicles on the huge red, circular roof tank of the laundry across the alley, the clear sky, when he discovered that a sentiment was approaching. It was said of him, occasionally, that he did not love anyone. This was not true. He did not love anyone steadily. But unsteadily he loved, he guessed, at an average rate.

The sentiment, as he drank his coffee, was for two cousins in upstate New York, the Mohawk Valley. They were dead. Isaac Braun and his sister Tina. Tina was first to go. Two years later, Isaac died. Braun now discovered that he and Cousin Isaac had loved each other. For whatever use or meaning this fact might have within the peculiar system of light, movement, contact, and perishing in which he tried to find stability. Toward Tina, Dr. Braun's feelings were less clear. More passionate once, but at present more detached.

Isaac's wife, after he died, had told Braun, "He was proud of you. He said, 'Sammy has been written up in *Time,* in all the papers, for his research. But he never says a word about his scientific reputation!' "

"I see. Well, computers do the work, actually."

"But you have to know what to put into these computers."

This was more or less the case. But Braun had not continued the conversation. He did not care much for being *first* in his field. People were boastful in America. Matthew Arnold, a not entirely appetizing figure himself, had correctly observed this in the U.S. Dr. Braun thought this native American boastfulness had aggravated a certain weakness in Jewish immigrants. But a proportionate reaction of self-effacement was not praiseworthy. Dr. Braun did not want to be interested in this question at all. However, his cousin Isaac's opinions had some value for him.

In Schenectady there were two more Brauns of the same family, living. Did Dr. Braun, drinking his coffee this afternoon, love them, too? They did not elicit such feelings. Then did he love Isaac more because Isaac was dead? There one might have something.

But in childhood, Isaac had shown him great kindness. The others, not very much.

Now Braun remembered certain things. A sycamore tree
beside the Mohawk River. Then the river couldn't have been
so foul. Its color, anyhow, was green, and it was powerful
and dark, an easy, level force—crimped, green, blackish,
glassy. A huge tree like a complicated event, with much
splitting and thick chalky extensions. It must have dominated an acre, brown and white. And well away from the
leaves, on a dead branch, sat a gray-and-blue fish hawk.
Isaac and his little cousin Braun passed in the wagon—
the old coarse-tailed horse walking, the steady head in
blinders, working onward. Braun, seven years old, wore a
gray shirt with large bone buttons and had a short summer
haircut. Isaac was dressed in work clothes, for in those
days the Brauns were in the secondhand business—furniture, carpets, stoves, beds. His senior by fifteen years, Isaac
had a mature business face. Born to be a man, in the direct
Old Testament sense, as that bird on the sycamore was
born to fish in water. Isaac, when he had come to America,
was still a child. Nevertheless his old-country Jewish dignity was very firm and strong. He had the outlook of ancient generations on the New World. Tents and kine and
wives and maidservants and manservants. Isaac was
handsome, Braun thought—dark face, black eyes, vigorous
hair, and a long scar on the cheek. Because, he told his
scientific cousin, his mother had given him milk from a
tubercular cow in the old country. While his father was
serving in the Russo-Japanese War. Far away. In the Yiddish metaphor, on the lid of hell. As though hell were a
caldron, a covered pot. How those old-time Jews despised
the goy wars, their vainglory and obstinate *Dummheit*.
Conscription, mustering, marching, shooting, leaving the
corpses everywhere. Buried, unburied. Army against army.
Gog and Magog. The czar, that weak, whiskered arbitrary
and woman-ridden man, decreed that Uncle Braun would
be swept away to Sakhalin. So by irrational decree, as

in *The Arabian Nights*, Uncle Braun, with his greatcoat and short humiliated legs, little beard, and great eyes, left wife and child to eat maggoty pork. And when the War was lost Uncle Braun escaped through Manchuria. Came to Vancouver on a Swedish ship. Labored on the railroad. He did not look so strong, as Braun remembered him in Schenectady. His chest was deep and his arms long, but the legs like felt, too yielding, as if the escape from Sakhalin and trudging in Manchuria had been too much. However, in the Mohawk Valley, monarch of used stoves and fumigated mattresses—dear Uncle Braun! He had a small, pointed beard, like George V, like Nick of Russia. Like Lenin, for that matter. But large, patient eyes in his wizened face, filling all of the space reserved for eyes.

A vision of mankind Braun was having as he sat over his coffee Saturday afternoon. Beginning with those Jews of 1920.

Braun as a young child was protected by the special affection of his cousin Isaac, who stroked his head and took him on the wagon, later the truck, into the countryside. When Braun's mother had gone into labor with him, it was Isaac whom Aunt Rose sent running for the doctor. He found the doctor in the saloon. Faltering, drunken Jones, who practiced among Jewish immigrants before those immigrants had educated their own doctors. He had Isaac crank the Model T. And they drove. Arriving, Jones tied Mother Braun's hands to the bedposts, a custom of the times.

Having worked as a science student in laboratories and kennels, Dr. Braun had himself delivered cats and dogs. Man, he knew, entered life like these other creatures, in a transparent bag or caul. Lying in a bag filled with transparent fluid, a purplish water. A color to mystify the most rational philosopher. What is this creature that struggles for birth in its membrane and clear fluid? Any puppy in its

sac, in the blind terror of its emergence, any mouse breaking into the external world from this shining, innocent-
seeming blue-tinged transparency!

Dr. Braun was born in a small wooden house. They
washed him and covered him with mosquito netting. He lay
at the foot of his mother's bed. Tough Cousin Isaac dearly
loved Braun's mother. He had great pity for her. In inter-
vals of his dealing, of being a Jewish businessman, there
fell these moving reflections of those who were dear to him.

Aunt Rose was Dr. Braun's godmother, held him at his
circumcision. Bearded, nearsighted old Krieger, fingers
stained with chicken slaughter, cut away the foreskin.

Aunt Rose, Braun felt, was the original dura mater—the
primal hard mother. She was not a big woman. She had a
large bust, wide hips, and old-fashioned thighs of those
corrupted shapes that belong to history. Which hampered
her walk. Together with poor feet, broken by the excessive
female weight she carried. In old boots approaching the
knee. Her face was red, her hair powerful, black. She had a
straight sharp nose. To cut mercy like a cotton thread. In
the light of her eyes Braun recognized the joy she took in
her hardness. Hardness of reckoning, hardness of tactics,
hardness of dealing and of speech. She was building a
kingdom with the labor of Uncle Braun and the strength of
her obedient sons. They had their shop, they had real estate. They had a hideous synagogue of such red brick as
seemed to grow in upstate New York by the will of the
demon spirit charged with the ugliness of America in that
epoch, which saw to it that a particular comic ugliness
should influence the soul of man. In Schenectady, in Troy,
in Gloversville, Mechanicville, as far west as Buffalo. There
was a sour paper mustiness in this synagogue. Uncle Braun
not only had money, he also had some learning and he was
respected. But it was a quarrelsome congregation. Every
question was disputed. There was rivalry, there were rages;
slaps were given, families stopped speaking. Pariahs,

thought Braun, with the dignity of princes among themselves.

Silent, with silent eyes crossing and recrossing the red water tank bound by twisted cables, from which ragged ice hung down and white vapor rose, Dr. Braun extracted a moment four decades gone in which Cousin Isaac had said, with one of those archaic looks he had, that the Brauns were descended from the tribe of Naphtali.

"How do we know?"

"People—families—*know*."

Braun was reluctant, even at the age of ten, to believe such things. But Isaac, with the authority of a senior, almost an uncle, said, "You'd better not forget it."

As a rule, he was gay with young Braun. Laughing against the tension of the scar that forced his mouth to one side. His eyes black, soft, and flaming. Off his breath, a bitter fragrance that translated itself to Braun as masculine earnestness and gloom. All the sons in the family had the same sort of laugh. They sat on the open porch, Sundays, laughing, while Uncle Braun read aloud the Yiddish matrimonial advertisements. "Attractive widow, 35, dark-favored, owning her own dry-goods business in Hudson, excellent cook, Orthodox, well-bred, refined. Plays the piano. Two intelligent, well-behaved children, eight and six."

All but Tina, the obese sister, took part in this satirical Sunday pleasure. Behind the screen door, she stood in the kitchen. Below, the yard, where crude flowers grew—zinnias, plantain lilies, trumpet vine on the chicken shed.

Now the country cottage appeared to Braun, in the Adirondacks. A stream. So beautiful! Trees, full of great strength. Wild strawberries, but you must be careful about the poison ivy. In the drainage ditches, polliwogs. Braun slept in the attic with Cousin Mutt. Mutt danced in his undershirt in the morning, naked beneath, and sang an obscene song:

"I stuck my nose up a nanny goat's ass
And the smell was enough to blind me."

He was leaping on bare feet, and his thing bounded from thigh to thigh. Going into saloons to collect empty bottles, he had learned this. A ditty from the stokehold. Origin, Liverpool or Tyneside. Art of the laboring class in the machine age.

An old mill. A pasture with clover flowers. Braun, seven years old, tried to make a clover wreath, pinching out a hole in the stems for other stems to pass through. He meant the wreath for fat Tina. To put it on her thick savory head, her smoky black harsh hair. Then in the pasture, little Braun overturned a rotten stump with his foot. Hornets pursued and bit him. He screamed. He had painful crimson lumps all over his body. Aunt Rose put him to bed and Tina came huge into the attic to console him. An angry fat face, black eyes, and the dilated nose breathing at him. Little Braun, stung and burning. She lifted her dress and petticoat to cool him with her body. The belly and thighs swelled before him. Braun felt too small and frail for this ecstasy. By the bedside was a chair, and she sat. Under the dizzy heat of the shingled roof, she rested her legs upon him, spread them wider, wider. He saw the barbarous and coaly hair. He saw the red within. She parted the folds with her fingers. Parting, her dark nostrils opened, the eyes looked white in her head. She motioned that he should press his child's genital against her fat-flattened thighs. Which, with agonies of incapacity and pleasure, he did. All was silent. Summer silence. Her sexual odor. The flies and gnats stimulated by delicious heat or the fragrance. He heard a mass of flies tear themselves from the windowpane. A sound of detached adhesive. Tina did not kiss, did not embrace. Her face was menacing. She was defying. She was drawing him—taking him somewhere with her. But she promised nothing, told him nothing.

When he recovered from his bites, playing once more in the yard, Braun saw Isaac with his fiancée, Clara Sternberg, walking among the trees, embracing very sweetly. Braun tried to go with them, but Cousin Isaac sent him away. When he still followed, Cousin Isaac turned him roughly toward the cottage. Little Braun then tried to kill his cousin. He wanted with all his heart to club Isaac with a piece of wood. He was still struck by the incomparable happiness, the luxury of that pure murderousness. Rushing toward Isaac, who took him by the back of the neck, twisted his head, held him under the pump. He then decreed that little Braun must go home, to Albany. He was far too wild. Must be taught a lesson. Cousin Tina said in private, "Good for *you*, Sam. I hate him, too." She took Braun with her dimpled, inept hand and walked down the road with him in the Adirondack dust. Her gingham-fitted bulk. Her shoulders curved, banked, like the earth of the hill-cut road. And her feet turned outward by the terrifying weight and deformity of her legs.

Later she dieted. Became for a while thinner, more civilized. Everyone was more civilized. Little Braun became a docile, bookish child. Did very well at school.

All clear? Quite clear to the adult Braun, considering his fate no more than the fate of others. Before his tranquil look, the facts arranged themselves—rose, took a new arrangement. Remained awhile in the settled state and then changed again. We were getting somewhere.

Uncle Braun died angry with Aunt Rose. He turned his face to the wall with his last breath to rebuke her hardness. All the men, his sons, burst out weeping. The tears of the women were different. Later, too, their passion took other forms. They bargained for more property. And Aunt Rose defied Uncle Braun's will. She collected rents in the slums of Albany and Schenectady from properties he had left to his sons. She dressed herself in the old fashion, calling on nigger tenants or the Jewish rabble of tailors and cobblers.

To her the old Jewish words for these trades—*Schneider*, *Schuster*—were terms of contempt. Rents belonging mainly to Isaac she banked in her own name. Riding ancient streetcars in the factory slums. She did not need to buy widow's clothes. She had always worn suits, they had always been black. Her hat was three-cornered, like the town crier's. She let the black braid hang behind, as though she were in her own kitchen. She had trouble with bladder and arteries, but ailments did not keep her at home and she had no use for doctoring and drugs. She blamed Uncle Braun's death on Bromo-Seltzer, which, she said, had enlarged his heart.

Isaac did not marry Clara Sternberg. Though he was a manufacturer, her father turned out on inquiry to have started as a cutter and have married a housemaid. Aunt Rose would not tolerate such a connection. She took long trips to make genealogical investigations. And she vetoed all the young women, her judgments severe without limit. "A false dog." "Candied poison." "An open ditch. A sewer. A born whore!"

The woman Isaac eventually married was pleasant, mild, round, respectable, the daughter of a Jewish farmer.

Aunt Rose said, "Ignorant. A common man."

"He's honest, a hard worker on the land," said Isaac. "He recites the Psalms even when he's driving. He keeps them under his wagon seat."

"I don't believe it. A son of Ham like that. A cattle dealer. He stinks of manure." And she said to the bride in Yiddish, "Be so good as to wash thy father before bringing him to the synagogue. Get a bucket and scalding water, and 20 Mule Team Borax and ammonia, and a horse brush. The filth is ingrained. Be sure to scrub his hands."

The rigid madness of the Orthodox. Their haughty, spinning, crazy spirit.

Tina did not bring her young man from New York to be

examined by Aunt Rose. Anyway, he was neither young, nor handsome, nor rich. Aunt Rose said he was a minor hoodlum, a slugger. She had gone to Coney Island to inspect his family—a father who sold pretzels and chestnuts from a cart, a mother who cooked for banquets. And the groom himself—so thick, so bald, so grim, she said, his hands so common and his back and chest like fur, a fell. He was a beast, she told young Sammy Braun. Braun was a student then at Rensselaer Polytechnic and came to see his aunt in her old kitchen—the great black-and-nickel stove, the round table on its oak pedestal, the dark-blue-and-white check of the oilcloth, a still life of peaches and cherries salvaged from the secondhand shop. And Aunt Rose, more feminine with her corset off and a gaudy wrapper over her thick Victorian undervests, camisoles, bloomers. Her silk stockings were gartered below the knee and the wide upper portions, fashioned for thighs, drooped down flimsy, nearly to her slippers.

Tina was then handsome, if not pretty. In high school she took off eighty pounds. Then she went to New York City without getting her diploma. What did *she* care for such things! said Rose. And how did she get to Coney Island by herself? Because she was perverse. Her instinct was for freaks. And there she met this beast. This hired killer, this second Lepke of Murder, Inc. Upstate, the old woman read the melodramas of the Yiddish press, which she embroidered with her own ideas of wickedness.

But when Tina brought her husband to Schenectady, installing him in her father's secondhand shop, he turned out to be a big innocent man. If he had ever had guile, he lost it with his hair. His baldness was total, like a purge. He had a sentimental, dependent look. Tina protected him. Here Dr. Braun had sexual thoughts, about himself as a child and about her childish bridegroom. And scowling, smoldering Tina, her angry tenderness in the Adirondacks, and how she was beneath, how hard she breathed in the attic, and the violent strength and obstinacy of her crinkled, sooty hair.

Nobody could sway Tina. That, thought Braun, was probably the secret of it. She had consulted her own will, kept her own counsel for so long, that she could accept no outer guidance. Anyone who listened to others seemed to her weak.

When Aunt Rose lay dead, Tina took from her hand the ring Isaac had given her many years ago. Braun did not remember the entire history of that ring, only that Isaac had loaned money to an immigrant who disappeared, leaving this jewel, which was assumed to be worthless but turned out to be valuable. Braun could not recall whether it was ruby or emerald; nor the setting. But it was the one feminine adornment Aunt Rose wore. And it was supposed to go to Isaac's wife, Sylvia, who wanted it badly. Tina took it from the corpse and put it on her own finger.

"Tina, give that ring to me. Give it here," said Isaac.

"No. It was hers. Now it's mine."

"It was not Mama's. You know that. Give it back."

She outfaced him over the body of Aunt Rose. She knew he would not quarrel at the deathbed. Sylvia was enraged. She did what she could. That is, she whispered, "Make her!" But it was no use. He knew he could not recover it. Besides, there were too many other property disputes. His rents in Aunt Rose's savings bank.

But only Isaac became a millionaire. The others simply hoarded, old immigrant style. He never sat waiting for his legacy. By the time Aunt Rose died, Isaac was already worth a great deal of money. He had put up an ugly apartment building in Albany. To him, an achievement. He was out with his men at dawn. Having prayed aloud while his wife, in curlers, pretty but puffy with sleepiness, sleepy but obedient, was in the kitchen fixing breakfast. Isaac's Orthodoxy only increased with his wealth. He soon became an old-fashioned Jewish paterfamilias. With his family he spoke a Yiddish unusually thick in old Slavic and Hebrew expressions. Instead of "important people, leading citizens," he said *"Anshe ha-ir,"* Men of the City. He, too, kept the Psalms near. As active, worldly Jews for centuries had done. One copy lay in the glove compartment of his Cadillac. To which his great gloomy sister referred with a twist of the face—she had become obese again, wider and taller, since those Adirondack days. She said, "He reads the Tehillim aloud in his air-conditioned Caddy when there's a long freight train at the crossing. That crook! He'd pick God's pocket!"

One could not help thinking what fertility of metaphor there was in all of these Brauns. Dr. Braun himself was no exception. And what the explanation might be, despite twenty-five years of specialization in the chemistry of heredity, he couldn't say. How a protein molecule might carry such propensities of ingenuity, and creative malice and negative power. Originating in an invisible ferment. Capable of printing a talent or a vice upon a billion hearts. No wonder Isaac Braun cried out to his God when he sat sealed in his great black car and the freights rumbled in the polluted shimmering of this once-beautiful valley

> Answer me when I call, O God of my
> righteousness.

"But what do you think?" said Tina. "Does he remember his brothers when there is a deal going? Does he give his only sister a chance to come in?"

Not that there was any great need. Cousin Mutt, after he was wounded at Iwo Jima, returned to the appliance business. Cousin Aaron was a C.P.A. Tina's husband, bald Fenster, branched into housewares in his secondhand shop. Tina was back of that, of course. No one was poor. What irritated Tina was that Isaac would not carry the family into real estate, where the tax advantages were greatest.

The big depreciation allowances, which she understood as
legally sanctioned graft. She had her money in savings accounts at a disgraceful two and a half percent, taxed at the
full rate. She did not trust the stock market.

Isaac had tried, in fact, to include the Brauns when he
built the shopping center at Robbstown. At a risky moment,
they abandoned him. A desperate moment, when the law
had to be broken. At a family meeting, each of the Brauns
had agreed to put up $25,000, the entire amount to be
given under the table to Ilkington. Old Ilkington headed the
board of directors of the Robbstown Country Club. Sur-
rounded by factories, the club was moving farther into the
country. Isaac had learned this from the old caddie master
when he gave him a lift, one morning of fog. Mutt Braun
had caddied at Robbstown in the early twenties, had carried Ilkington's clubs. Isaac knew Ilkington, too, and had a
private talk with him. The old goy, now seventy, retiring to
the British West Indies, had said to Isaac, "Off the record.
One hundred thousand. And I don't want to bother about
Internal Revenue." He was a long, austere man with a mar-
bled face. Cornell 1910 or so. Cold but plain. And, in
Isaac's opinion, fair. Developed as a shopping center, properly planned, the Robbstown golf course was worth half a
million apiece to the Brauns. The city in the postwar boom
was spreading fast. Isaac had a friend on the zoning board
who would clear everything for five grand. As for the con-
tracting, he offered to do it all on his own. Tina insisted
that a separate corporation be formed by the Brauns to
make sure the building profits were shared equally. To this
Isaac agreed. As head of the family, he took the burden
upon himself. He would have to organize it all. Only Aaron
the C.P.A. could help him, setting up the books. The meeting, in Aaron's office, lasted from noon to three P.M. All the
difficult problems were examined. Four players, specialists
in the harsh music of money, studying a score. In the end,
they agreed to perform.

But when the time came, ten A.M. on a Friday, Aaron balked. He would not do it. And Tina and Mutt also reneged. Isaac told Dr. Braun the story. As arranged, he came to Aaron's office carrying the $25,000 for Ilkington in an old briefcase. Aaron, now forty, smooth, shrewd, and dark, had the habit of writing tiny neat numbers on his memo pad as he spoke to you. Dark fingers quickly consulting the latest tax publications. He dropped his voice very low to the secretary on the intercom. He wore white-on-white shirts and silk-brocade ties, signed "Countess Mara." Of them all, he looked most like Uncle Braun. But without the beard, without the kingly pariah derby, without the gold thread in his brown eye. In many externals, thought scientific Braun, Aaron and Uncle Braun were drawn from the same genetic pool. Chemically, he was the younger brother of his father. The differences within were due possibly to heredity. Or perhaps to the influence of business America.

"Well?" said Isaac, standing in the carpeted office. The grandiose desk was superbly clean.

"How do you know Ilkington can be trusted?"

"I think he can."

"*You* think. He could take the money and say he never heard of you in all his life."

"Yes, he might. But we talked that over. We have to gamble."

Probably on his instructions, Aaron's secretary buzzed him. He bent over the instrument and out of the corner of his mouth he spoke to her very deliberately and low.

"Well, Aaron," said Isaac. "You want me to guarantee your investment? Well? Speak up."

Aaron had long ago subdued his thin tones and spoke in the gruff style of a man always sure of himself. But the sharp breaks, mastered twenty-five years ago, were still there. He stood up with both fists on the glass of his desk, trying to control his voice.

He said through clenched teeth, "I haven't slept!"

"Where is the money?"

"I don't have that kind of cash."

"No?"

"You know damn well. I'm licensed. I'm a certified accountant. I'm in no position . . ."

"And what about Tina—Mutt?"

"I don't know anything about them."

"Talked them out of it, didn't you? I have to meet Ilkington at noon. Sharp. Why didn't you tell me sooner?"

Aaron said nothing.

Isaac dialed Tina's number and let the phone ring. Certain that she was there, gigantically listening to the steely, beady drilling of the telephone. He let it ring, he said, about five minutes. He made no effort to call Mutt. Mutt would do as Tina did.

"I have an hour to raise this dough."

"In my bracket," Aaron said, "the twenty-five would cost me more than fifty."

"You could have told me this yesterday. Knowing what it means to me."

"You'll turn over a hundred thousand to a man you don't know? Without a receipt? Blind? Don't do it."

But Isaac had decided. In our generation, Dr. Braun thought, a sort of playboy capitalist has emerged. He gaily takes a flier in rebuilt office machinery for Brazil, motels in East Africa, high-fidelity components in Thailand. A hundred thousand means little. He jets down with a chick to see the scene. The governor of a province is waiting in his Thunderbird to take the guests on jungle expressways built by graft and peons to a surf-and-champagne weekend where the executive, youthful at fifty, closes the deal. But Cousin Isaac had put his stake together penny by penny, old style, starting with rags and bottles as a boy; then fire-salvaged goods; then used cars; then learning the building trades. Earth moving, foundations, concrete, sewage, wir-

ing, roofing, heating systems. He got his money the hard
way. And now he went to the bank and borrowed $75,000,
at full interest. Without security, he gave it to Ilkington in
Ilkington's parlor. Furnished in old goy taste and dissemi-
nating an old goy odor of tiresome, silly, respectable things.
Of which Ilkington was clearly so proud. The applewood,
the cherry, the wing tables and cabinets, the upholstery
with a flavor of dry paste, the pork-pale colors of gentility.
Ilkington did not touch Isaac's briefcase. He did not intend,
evidently, to count the bills, nor even to look. He offered
Isaac a martini. Isaac, not a drinker, drank the clear gin. At
noon. Like something distilled in outer space. Having no
color. He sat there sturdily, but felt lost—lost to his people,
his family, lost to God, lost in the void of America. Ilkington drank a shaker of cocktails, gentlemanly, stony, like a
high slab of something generically human, but with few
human traits familiar to Isaac. At the door he did not say
he would keep his word. He simply shook hands with Isaac,
saw him to the car. Isaac drove home and sat in the den of
his bungalow. Two whole days. Then on Monday, Ilkington
phoned to say that the Robbstown directors had decided to
accept his offer for the property. A pause. Then Ilkington
added that no written instrument could replace trust and
decency between gentlemen.

Isaac took possession of the country club and filled it
with a shopping center. All such places are ugly. Dr. Braun
could not say why this one struck him as especially brutal
in its ugliness. Perhaps because he remembered the Robbstown Club. Restricted, of course. But Jews could look at it
from the road. And the elms had been lovely—a century or
older. The light, delicate. And the Coolidge-era sedans turning in, with small curtains at the rear window, and holders
for artificial flowers. Hudsons, Auburns, Bearcats. Only
machinery. Nothing to feel nostalgic about.

Still, Braun was startled to see what Isaac had done. Perhaps in an unconscious assertion of triumph—in the vividness of victory. The green acres reserved, it was true, for mild idleness, for hitting a little ball with a stick, were now paralyzed by parking for five hundred cars. Supermarket, pizza joint, chop suey, laundromat, Robert Hall clothes, a dime store.

And this was only the beginning. Isaac became a millionaire. He filled the Mohawk Valley with housing developments. And he began to speak of "my people," meaning those who lived in the buildings he had raised. He was stingy with land, he built too densely, it was true, but he built with benevolence. At six in the morning, he was out with his crews. He lived very simply. Walked humbly with his God, as the rabbi said. A Madison Avenue rabbi, by this time. The little synagogue was wiped out. It was as dead as the Dutch painters who would have appreciated its dimness and its shaggy old peddlers. Now there was a *temple* like a World's Fair pavilion. Isaac was president, having beaten out the father of a famous hoodlum, once executioner for the Mob in the Northeast. The worldly rabbi with his trained voice and tailored suits, like a Christian minister except for the play of Jewish cleverness in his face, hinted to the old-fashioned part of the congregation that he had to pour it on for the sake of the young people. America. Extraordinary times. If you wanted the young women to bless Sabbath candles, you had to start their rabbi at $20,000, and add a house and a Jaguar.

Cousin Isaac, meantime, grew more old-fashioned. His car was ten years old. But he was a strong sort of man. Self-assured, a dark head scarcely thinning at the top. Upstate women said he gave out the positive male energy they were beginning to miss in men. He had it. It was in the manner with which he picked up a fork at the table, the way he poured from a bottle. Of course, the world had done for him exactly what he had demanded. That meant he had made the right demand and in the right place. It meant his reading of life was metaphysically true. Or that the Old Testament, the Talmud, and Polish Ashkenazi Orthodoxy were irresistible.

But that wouldn't altogether do, thought Dr. Braun. There was more there than piety. He recalled his cousin's white teeth and scar-twisted smile when he was joking. "I fought on many fronts," Cousin Isaac said, meaning women's bellies. He often had a sound American way of putting things. Had known the back stairs in Schenectady that led to the sheets, the gripping arms and spreading thighs of workingwomen. The Model T was parked below. Earlier, the horse waited in harness. He got great pleasure from masculine reminiscences. Recalling Dvorah the greenhorn, on her knees, hiding her head in pillows while her buttocks soared, a burst of kinky hair from the walls of whiteness, and her feeble voice crying, *"Nein."* But she did not mean it.

Cousin Mutt had no such anecdotes. Shot in the head at Iwo Jima, he came back from a year in the hospital to sell Zenith, Motorola, and Westinghouse appliances. He married a respectable girl and went on quietly amid a bewildering expansion and transformation of his birthplace. A computer center taking over the bush-league park where a scout had him spotted before the war as material for the majors. On most important matters, Mutt went to Tina. She told him what to do. And Isaac looked out for him, whenever possible buying appliances through Mutt for his housing developments. But Mutt took his problems to Tina. For instance, his wife and her sister played the horses. Every chance they got, they drove to Saratoga, to the trotting races. Probably no great harm in this. The two sisters with gay lipstick and charming dresses. And laughing continually with their pretty jutting teeth. And putting down the top of the convertible.

Tina took a mild view of this. Why shouldn't they go to the track? Her fierceness was concentrated, all of it, on Braun the millionaire.

"That whoremaster!" she said.

"Oh, no. Not in years and years," said Mutt.

"Come, Mutt. I know whom he's been balling. I keep an eye on the Orthodox. Believe me, I do. And now the governor has put him on a commission. Which is it?"

"Pollution."

"Water pollution, that's right. Rockefeller's buddy."

"Well, you shouldn't, Tina. He's our brother."

"He feels for *you*."

"Yes, he does."

"A multimillionaire—lets you go on drudging in a little business? He's heartless. A heartless man."

"It's not true."

"What? He never had a tear in his eye unless the wind was blowing," said Tina.

Hyperbole was Tina's greatest weakness. They were all like that. The mother had bred it in them.

Otherwise, she was simply a gloomy, obese woman, sternly combed, the hair tugged back from her forehead, tight, so that the hairline was a fighting barrier. She had a totalitarian air. And not only toward others. Toward herself, also. Absorbed in the dictatorship of her huge person. In a white dress, and with the ring on her finger she had seized from her dead mother. By a *putsch* in the bedroom.

In her generation—Dr. Braun had given up his afternoon to the hopeless pleasure of thinking affectionately about his dead—in her generation, Tina was also old-fashioned for all her modern slang. People of her sort, and not only the women, cultivated charm. But Tina willed consistently to appeal for nothing, to have no charm. Absolutely none. She never tried to please. Her aim must have been majesty. Based on what? She had no great thoughts. She built on her own nature. On a primordial idea, hugely blown up. Somewhat as her flesh in its dress of white silk, as last seen by Cousin Braun some years ago, was blown up. Some sub-suboffice of the personality, behind a little door of the brain where the restless spirit never left its work, had ordered this tremendous female form, all of it, to become manifest, with dark hair on the forearms, conspicuous nostrils in the white face, and black eyes staring. The eyes had an affronted expression; sometimes a look of sulphur; a clever look—they had all the looks, even the look of kindness that came from Uncle Braun. The old man's sweetness. Those who try to interpret humankind through its eyes are in for much strangeness—perplexity.

The quarrel between Tina and Isaac lasted for years. She accused him of shaking off the family when the main chance came. He had refused to cut them in. He said that they had all deserted him at the zero hour. Eventually, the brothers made it up. Not Tina. She wanted nothing to do with Isaac. In the first phase of enmity she saw to it that he should know exactly what she thought of him. Brothers, aunts, and old friends reported what she was saying about him. He was a crook. Mama had lent him money; he would not repay; that was why she had collected those rents. Also, Isaac had been a silent partner of Zaikas, the Greek, the racketeer from Troy. She said that Zaikas had covered for Isaac, who was implicated in the state-hospital scandal. Zaikas took the fall, but Isaac had to put $50,000 in Zaikas's box at the bank. The Stuyvesant Bank, that was. Tina said she even knew the box number. Isaac said little to these slanders, and after a time they stopped.

And it was when they stopped that Isaac actually began to feel the anger of his sister. He felt it as head of the family, the oldest living Braun. After he had not seen his sister for two or three years, he began to remind himself of Uncle Braun's affection for Tina. The only daughter. The youngest. Our baby sister. Thoughts of the old days touched his heart. Having gotten what he wanted, Tina said to Mutt, he could redo the past in sentimental colors. Isaac would remember that in 1920 Aunt Rose wanted fresh milk, and the Brauns kept a cow in the pasture by the river. What a beautiful place. And how delicious it was to crank the Model T and drive at dusk to milk the cow beside the green water. Driving, they sang songs. Tina, then ten years old, must have weighed two hundred pounds, but the shape of her mouth was very sweet, womanly—perhaps the pressure of the fat, hastening her maturity. Somehow she was more feminine in childhood than later. It was true that at nine or ten she sat on a kitten in the rocker, unaware, and smothered it. Aunt Rose found it dead when her daughter stood up. "You huge thing," she said to her daughter, "you animal." But even this Isaac recollected with amused sadness. And since he belonged to no societies, never played cards, never spent an evening drinking, never went to Florida, never went to Europe, never went to see the State of Israel, Isaac had plenty of time for reminiscences. Respectable elms about his house sighed with him for the past. The squirrels were orthodox. They dug and saved. Mrs. Isaac Braun wore no cosmetics. Except a touch of lipstick when going out in public. No mink coats. A comfortable Hudson seal, yes. With a large fur button on the belly. To keep her, as he liked her, warm. Fair, pale, round, with a steady innocent look, and hair worn short and symmetrical. Light brown, with kinks of gold. One gray eye, perhaps, expressed or came near expressing slyness. It must have been purely involuntary. At least there was not the slightest sign of conscious criticism or opposition. Isaac was master. Cooking, baking, laundry, all housekeeping, had to meet his standard. If he didn't like the smell of the cleaning woman, she was sent away. It was an ample plain old-fashioned respectable domestic life on an Eastern European model completely destroyed in 1939 by Hitler and Stalin. Those two saw to the eradication of the old condi-

tions, made sure that certain modern concepts became social realities. Maybe the slightest troubling ambiguity in
one of Cousin Sylvia's eyes was the effect of a suppressed
historical comment. As a woman, Dr. Braun considered, she
had more than a glimmering of this modern transformation. Her husband was a multimillionaire. Where was the
life this might have bought? The houses, servants, clothes,
and cars? On the farm she had operated machines. As his
wife, she was obliged to forget how to drive. She was a
docile, darling woman, and she was in the kitchen baking
spongecake and chopping liver, as Isaac's mother had
done. Or should have done. Without the flaming face, the
stern meeting brows, the rigorous nose, and the club of
powerful braid lying on her spine. Without Aunt Rose's
curses.

In America, the abuses of the Old World were righted. It
was appointed to be the land of historical redress. However, Dr. Braun reflected, new uproars filled the soul. Material details were of the greatest importance. But still the
largest strokes were made by the spirit. Had to be! People
who said this were right.

Cousin Isaac's thoughts: a web of computations, of
frontages, elevations, drainage, mortgages, turn-around
money. And since, in addition, he had been a strong,
raunchy young man, and this had never entirely left him
(it remained only as witty comment), his piety really
did appear to be put on. Superadded. The Psalm-saying at
building sites. *When I consider the heavens, the work of
Thy fingers . . . what is Man that Thou art mindful of
him?* But he evidently meant it all. He took off whole afternoons before high holidays. While his fair-faced wife,
flushed with baking, noted with the slightly Biblical air he
expected of her that he was bathing, changing upstairs. He
had visited the graves of his parents. Announcing, "I've
been to the cemetery."

"Oh," she said with sympathy, the one beautiful eye full of candor. The other fluttering with a minute quantity of slyness.

The parents, stifled in the clay. Two crates, side by side. Grass of burning green sweeping over them, and Isaac repeating a prayer to the God of Mercy. And in Hebrew with a Baltic accent at which modern Israelis scoffed. September trees, yellow after an icy night or two, now that the sky was blue and warm, gave light instead of shadow. Isaac was concerned about his parents. Down there, how were they? The wet, the cold, above all the worms worried him. In frost, his heart shrank for Aunt Rose and Uncle Braun, though as a builder he knew they were beneath the frost line. But a human power, his love, affected his practical judgment. It flew off. Perhaps as a builder and housing expert (on two of the governor's commissions, not one) he especially felt his dead to be unsheltered. But Tina—they were her dead, too—felt he was still exploiting Papa and Mama and that he would have exploited her, too, if she had let him.

For several years, at the same season, there was a scene between them. The pious thing before the Day of Atonement was to visit the dead and to forgive the living—forgive and ask forgiveness. Accordingly, Isaac went annually to the old home. Parked his Cadillac. Rang the bell, his heart beating hard. He waited at the foot of the long, enclosed staircase. The small brick building, already old in 1915 when Uncle Braun had bought it, passed to Tina, who tried to make it modern. Her ideas came out of *House Beautiful*. The paper with which she covered the slanted walls of the staircase was unsuitable. It did not matter. Tina, above, opened the door, saw the masculine figure and scarred face of her brother and said, "What do you want?"

"Tina! For God's sake, I've come to make peace."

"What peace! You swindled us out of a fortune."

"The others don't agree. Now, Tina, we are brother and sister. Remember Father and Mother. Remember . . ."

She cried down at him, "You son of a bitch, I *do* remember! Now get the hell out of here."

Banging the door, she dialed her brother Aaron, lighting one of her long cigarettes. "He's been here again," she said. "What shit! He's not going to practice his goddamn religion on me."

She said she hated his Orthodox cringe. She could take him straight. In a deal. Or a swindle. But she couldn't bear his sentiment.

As for herself, she might smell like a woman, but she acted like a man. And in her dress, while swooning music came from the radio, she smoked her cigarette after he was gone, thundering inside with great flashes of feeling. For which, otherwise, there was no occasion. She might curse him, thought Dr. Braun, but she owed him much. Aunt Rose, who had been such a harsh poet of money, had left her daughter needs—such needs! Quiet middle-age domestic decency (husband, daughter, furnishings) did nothing for needs like hers.

So when Isaac Braun told his wife that he had visited the family graves, she knew that he had gone again to see Tina. The thing had been repeated. Isaac, with a voice and gesture that belonged to history and had no place or parallel in upstate industrial New York, appealed to his sister in the eyes of God, and in the name of souls departed, to end her anger. But she cried from the top of the stairs, "Never! You son of a bitch, never!" and he went away.

He went home for consolation, and walked to the synagogue later with an injured heart. A leader of the congregation, weighted with grief. Striking breast with fist in old-fashioned penitence. The new way was the way of understatement. Anglo-Saxon restraint. The rabbi, with his

Madison Avenue public-relations airs, did not go for these European Judaic, operatic fist-clenchings. Tears. He made the cantor tone it down. But Isaac Braun, covered by his father's prayer shawl with its black stripes and shedding fringes, ground his teeth and wept near the ark.

These annual visits to Tina continued until she became sick. When she went into the hospital, Isaac phoned Dr. Braun and asked him to find out how things really stood.

"But I'm not a medical doctor."

"You're a scientist. You'll understand it better."

Anyone might have understood. She was dying of cancer of the liver. Cobalt radiation was tried. Chemotherapy. Both made her very sick. Dr. Braun told Isaac, "There is no hope."

"I know."

"Have you seen her?"

"No. I hear from Mutt."

Isaac sent word through Mutt that he wanted to come to her bedside.

Tina refused to see him.

And Mutt, with his dark sloping face, unhandsome but gentle, dog-eyed, softly urged her, "You should, Tina."

But Tina said, "No. Why should I? A Jewish deathbed scene, that's what he wants. No."

"Come, Tina."

"No," she said, even firmer. Then she added, "I hate him." As though explaining that Mutt should not expect her to give up the support of this feeling. And a little later she added, in a lower voice, as though speaking generally, "I can't help him."

But Isaac phoned Mutt daily, saying, "I have to see my sister."

"I can't get her to do it."

"You've got to explain it to her. She doesn't know what's right."

Isaac even telephoned Fenster, though, as everyone was

aware, he had a low opinion of Fenster's intelligence. And Fenster answered, "She says you did us all dirt."

"I? She got scared and backed out. I had to go it alone."

"You shook us off."

Quite simple-mindedly, with the directness of the Biblical fool (this was how Isaac saw him, and Fenster knew it), he said, "You wanted it all for yourself, Isaac."

That they should let him, ungrudgingly, enjoy his great wealth, Isaac told Dr. Braun, was too much to expect. Of human beings. And he was very rich. He did not say how much money he had. This was a mystery in the family. The old people said, "He himself doesn't know."

Isaac confessed to Dr. Braun, "I never understood her." He was much moved, even then, a year later.

Cousin Tina had discovered that one need not be bound by the old rules. That, Isaac's painful longing to see his sister's face being denied, everything was put into a different sphere of advanced understanding, painful but truer than the old. From her bed she appeared to be directing this research.

"You ought to let him come," said Mutt.

"Because I'm dying?"

Mutt, plain and dark, stared at her, his black eyes momentarily vacant as he chose an answer. "People recover," he said.

But she said, with peculiar indifference to the fact, "Not this time." She had already become gaunt in the face and high in the belly. Her ankles were swelling. She had seen this in others and understood the signs.

"He calls every day," said Mutt.

She had had her nails done. A dark-red, almost maroon color. One of those odd twists of need or desire. The ring she had taken from her mother was now loose on the finger. And, reclining on the raised bed, as if she had found a moment of ease, she folded her arms and said, pressing the lace of the bed jacket with her finger tips, "Then give Isaac my message, Mutt. I'll see him, yes, but it'll cost him money."

"Money?"

"If he pays me twenty thousand dollars."

"Tina, that's not right."

"Why not! For my daughter. She'll need it."

"No, she doesn't need that kind of dough." He knew what Aunt Rose had left. "There's plenty and you know it."

"If he's got to come, that's the price of admission," she said. "Only a fraction of what he did us out of."

Mutt said simply, "He never did me out of anything." Curiously, the shrewdness of the Brauns was in his face, but he never practiced it. This was not because he had been wounded in the Pacific. He had always been like that. He sent Tina's message to Isaac on a piece of business stationery, BRAUN APPLIANCES, 42 CLINTON. Like a contract bid. No word of comment, not even a signature.

For 20 grand cash Tina says yes otherwise no.

In Dr. Braun's opinion, his Cousin Tina had seized upon the force of death to create a situation of opera. Which at the same time was a situation of parody. As he stated it to himself, there was a feedback of mockery. Death the horrid bridegroom, waiting with a consummation life had never offered. Life, accordingly, she devalued, filling up the clear light remaining (which should be reserved for beauty, miracle, nobility) with obese monstrosity, rancor, failure, self-torture.

Isaac, on the day he received Tina's terms, was scheduled to go out on the river with the governor's commission on pollution. A boat was sent by the Fish and Game Department to take the five members out on the Hudson. They would go south as far as Germantown. Where the river, with mountains on the west, seems a mile wide. And back again to Albany. Isaac would have canceled this inspection, he had so much thinking to do, was so full of things. "Overthronged" was the odd term Braun chose for it, which seemed to render Isaac's state best. But Isaac could not get out of this official excursion. His wife made him take his Panama hat and wear a light suit. He bent over the side of the boat, hands clasped tight on the dark-red, brass-jointed rail. He breathed through his teeth. At the back of his legs, in his neck, his pulses beating; and in the head an arterial swell through which he was aware, one-sidedly, of the air streaming, and gorgeous water. Two young professors from Rensselaer lectured on the geology and wildlife of the upper Hudson and on the industrial and community problems of the region. The towns were dumping raw sewage into the Mohawk and the Hudson. You could watch the flow from giant pipes. Cloacae, said the professor with his red beard and ruined teeth. Much dark metal in his mouth, pewter ridges instead of bone. And a pipe with which he pointed to the turds yellowing the river. The cities, spilling their filth. How dispose of it? Methods were discussed—treatment plants. Atomic power. And finally he presented an ingenious engineering project for sending all waste into the interior of the earth, far under the crust, thousands of feet into deeper strata. But even if pollution were stopped today, it would take fifty years to restore the river. The fish had persisted but at last abandoned their old spawning grounds. Only a savage scavenger eel dominated the water. The river great and blue in spite of the dung pools and the twisting of the eels.

One member of the governor's commission had a face remotely familiar, long and high, the mouth like a latch, cheeks hollow, the bone warped in the nose, and hair fading. Gentle. A thin person. His thoughts on Tina, Isaac had missed his name. But looking at the printed pages prepared by the staff, he saw that it was Ilkington Junior. This quiet, likable man examining him with such meaning from the white bulkhead, long trousers curling in the breeze as he held the metal rail behind him.

Evidently he knew about the $100,000.

"I think I was acquainted with your father," Isaac said, his voice very low.

"You were, indeed," said Ilkington. He was frail for his height; his skin was pulled tight, glistening on the temples, and a reddish blood lichen spread on his cheekbones. Capillaries. "The old man is well."

"Well. I'm glad."

"Yes. He's well. Very feeble. He had a bad time, you know."

"I never heard."

"Oh, yes, he invested in hotel construction in Nassau and lost his money."

"All of it?" said Isaac.

"All his legitimate money."

"I'm very sorry."

"Lucky he had a little something to fall back on."

"He did?"

"He certainly did."

"Yes, I see. That *was* lucky."

"It'll last him."

Isaac was glad to know and appreciated the kindness of Ilkington's son in telling him. Also the man knew what the Robbstown Country Club had been worth to him, but did not grudge him, behaved with courtesy. For which Isaac, filled with thankfulness, would have liked to show gratitude. But what you showed, among these people, you showed with silence. Of which, it seemed to Isaac, he was now beginning to appreciate the wisdom. The native, different wisdom of gentiles, who had much to say but refrained. What was this Ilkington Junior? He looked into the pages again and found a paragraph of biography. Insurance executive. Various government commissions. Probably Isaac could have discussed Tina with such a man. Yes, in heaven. On earth they would never discuss a thing. Silent impressions would have to do. Incommunicable diversities, kindly but silent contact. The more they had in their heads, the less people seemed to know how to tell it.

"When you write to your father, remember me to him."

Communities along the river, said the professor, would not pay for any sort of sewage-treatment plants. The Federal Government would have to arrange it. Only fair, Isaac considered, since Internal Revenue took away to Washington billions in taxes and left small change for the locals. So they pumped the excrements into the waterways. Isaac, building along the Mohawk, had always taken this for granted. Building squalid settlements of which he was so proud. . . . Had been proud.

He stepped onto the dock when the boat tied up. The State Game Commissioner had taken an eel from the water to show the inspection party. It was writhing toward the river in swift, powerful loops, tearing its skin on the planks, its crest of fin standing. *Treph!* And slimy black, the perishing mouth open.

The breeze had dropped and the wide water stank. Isaac drove home, turning on the air conditioner of his Cadillac. His wife said, "What was it like?"

He had no answer to give.

"What are you doing about Tina?"

Again, he said nothing.

But knowing Isaac, seeing how agitated he was, she predicted that he would go down to New York City for advice. She told this later to Dr. Braun, and he saw no reason to doubt it. Clever wives can foretell. A fortunate husband will be forgiven his predictability.

Isaac had a rabbi in Williamsburg. He was Orthodox enough for that. And he did not fly. He took a compartment on the Twentieth Century when it left Albany just before daybreak. With just enough light through the dripping gray to see the river. But not the west shore. A tanker covered by smoke and cloud divided the bituminous water. Presently the mountains emerged.

They wanted to take the old crack train out of service. The

carpets were filthy, the toilets stank. Slovenly waiters in the dining car. Isaac took toast and coffee, rejecting the odors of ham and bacon by expelling breath. Eating with his hat on. Racially distinct, as Dr. Braun well knew. A blood group characteristically eastern Mediterranean. The very fingerprints belonging to a distinctive family of patterns. The nose, the eyes long and full, the skin dark, slashed near the mouth by a Russian doctor in the old days. And looking out as they rushed past Rhinecliff, Isaac saw, with the familiarity of hundreds of journeys, the grand water, the thick trees—illuminated space. In the compartment, in captive leisure, shut up with the foul upholstery, the rattling door. The old arsenal, Bannerman's Island, the playful castle, yellow-green willows around it, and the water sparkling, as green as he remembered it in 1910— one of the forty million foreigners coming to America. The steel rails, as they were then, the twisting currents and the mountain round at the top, the wall of rock curving steeply into the expanding river.

From Grand Central, carrying a briefcase with all he needed in it, Isaac took the subway to his appointment. He waited in the anteroom, where the rabbi's bearded followers went in and out in long coats. Dressed in business clothes, Isaac, however, seemed no less archaic than the rest. A bare floor. Wooden seats, white stippled walls. But the windows were smeared, as though the outside did not matter. Of these people, many were survivors of the German holocaust. The rabbi himself had been through it as a boy. After the war, he had lived in Holland and Belgium and studied sciences in France. At Montpellier. Biochemistry. But he had been called—summoned—to these spiritual duties in New York; Isaac was not certain how this had happened. And now he wore the full beard. In his office, sitting at a little table with a green blotting pad, and a pen and note paper. The conversation was in the *jargón*—in Yiddish.

"Rabbi, my name is Isaac Braun."

"From Albany. Yes, I remember."

"I am the eldest of four—my sister, the youngest, the *muzínka*, is dying."

"Are you sure of this?"

"Of cancer of the liver, and with a lot of pain."

"Then she is. Yes, she is dying." From the very white, full face, the rabbi's beard grew straight and thick in rich bristles. He was a strong, youthful man, his stout body buttoned tightly, straining in the shiny black cloth.

"A certain thing happened soon after the war. An opportunity to buy a valuable piece of land for building. I invited my brothers and my sister to invest with me, Rabbi. But on the day . . ."

The rabbi listened, his white face lifted toward a corner of the ceiling, but fully attentive, his hands pressed to the ribs, above the waist.

"I understand. You tried to reach them that day. And you felt abandoned."

"They deserted me, Rabbi, yes."

"But that was also your good luck. They turned their faces from you, and this made you rich. You didn't have to share."

Isaac admitted this but added, "If it hadn't been one deal, it would have been another."

"You were destined to be rich?"

"I was sure to be. And there were so many opportunities."

"Your sister, poor thing, is very harsh. She is wrong. She has no ground for complaint against you."

"I am glad to hear that," said Isaac. "Glad," however, was only a word, for he was suffering.

"She is not a poor woman, your sister?"

"No, she inherited property. And her husband does pretty well. Though I suppose the long sickness costs."

"Yes, a wasting disease. But the living can only will to

live. I am speaking of Jews. They wanted to annihilate us. To give our consent would have been to turn from God. But about your problem: Have you thought of your brother Aaron? He advised the others not to take the risk."

"I know."

"It was to his interest that she should be angry with you, and not with him."

"I realize that."

"He is guilty. He is sinning against you. Your other brother is a good man."

"Mutt? Yes, I know. He is decent. He barely survived the war. He was shot in the head."

"But is he still himself?"

"Yes, I believe so."

"Sometimes it takes something like that. A bullet through the head." The rabbi paused and turned his round face, the black quill beard bent on the folds of shiny cloth. And then, as Isaac told him how he went to Tina before the high holidays, he looked impatient, moving his head forward, but his eyes turning sideward. "Yes. Yes." He was certain that Isaac had done the right things. "Yes. You have the money. She grudged you. Unreasonable. But that's how it seems to her. You are a man. She is only a woman. You are a rich man."

"But, Rabbi," said Isaac, "now she is on her deathbed, and I have asked to see her."

"Yes? Well?"

"She wants money for it."

"Ah? Does she? Money?"

"Twenty thousand dollars. So that I can be let into the room."

The burly rabbi was motionless, white fingers on the armrests of the wooden chair. "She knows she is dying, I suppose?" he said.

"Yes."

"Yes. Our Jews love deathbed jokes. I know many. Well.

America has not changed everything, has it? People assume that God has a sense of humor. Such jokes made by
the dying in anguish show a strong and brave soul, but
skeptical. What sort of woman is your sister?"

"Stout. Large."

"I see. A fat woman. A chunk of flesh with two eyes, as
they used to say. Staring at the lucky ones. Like an animal
in a cage, perhaps. Separated. By sensual greed and despair. A fat child like that—people sometimes behave as
though they were alone when such a child is present. So
those little monster souls have a strange fate. They see people as people are when no one is looking. A gloomy vision
of mankind."

Isaac respected the rabbi. Revered him, thought Dr.
Braun. But perhaps he was not old-fashioned enough for
him, notwithstanding the hat and beard and gabardine. He
had the old tones, the manner, the burly poise, the universal calm judgment of the Jewish moral genius. Enough to
satisfy anyone. But there was also something foreign about
him. That is, contemporary. Now and then there was a sign
of the science student, the biochemist from the south of
France, from Montpellier. He would probably have spoken
English with a French accent, whereas Cousin Isaac spoke
like anyone else from upstate. In Yiddish they had the
same dialect—White Russian. The Minsk region. The
Pripet Marshes, thought Dr. Braun. And then returned to
the fish hawk on the brown and chalky sycamore beside the
Mohawk. Yes. Perhaps. Among these recent birds, finches,
thrushes, there was Cousin Isaac with more scale than
feather in his wings. A more antique type. The ruddy brown
eye, the tough muscles of the jaw working under the skin.
Even the scar was precious to Dr. Braun. He knew the
man. Or rather, he had the longing of having known. For
these people were dead. A useless love.

"You can afford the money?" the rabbi asked. And when
Isaac hesitated, he said, "I don't ask you for the figure of

your fortune. It is not my concern. But could you give her the twenty thousand?"

And Isaac, looking greatly tried, said, "If I had to."

"It wouldn't make a great difference in your fortune?"

"No."

"In that case, why shouldn't you pay?"

"You think I should?"

"It's not for me to tell you to give away so much money. But you gave—you gambled—you trusted the man, the goy."

"Ilkington? That was a business risk. But Tina? So you believe I should pay?"

"Give in. I would say, judging the sister by the brother, there is no other way."

Then Isaac thanked him for his time and his opinion. He went out into the broad daylight of the street, which smelled of muck. The tedious mortar of tenements, settled out of line, the buildings sway-backed, with grime on grime, as if built of castoff shoes, not brick. The contractor observing. The ferment of sugar and roasting coffee was strong, but the summer air moved quickly in the damp under the huge machine-trampled bridge. Looking about for the subway entrance, Isaac saw instead a yellow cab with a yellow light on the crest. He first told the driver, "Grand Central," but changed his mind at the first corner and said, "Take me to the West Side Air Terminal." There was no fast train to Albany before late afternoon. He could not wait on Forty-second Street. Not today. He must have known all along that he would have to pay the money. He had come to get strength by consulting the rabbi. Old laws and wisdom on his side. But Tina from the deathbed had made too strong a move. If he refused to come across, no one could blame him. But he would feel greatly damaged. How would he live with himself? Because he made these sums easily now. Buying and selling a few city lots. Had the price been $50,000,

Tina would have been saying that he would never see her again. But $20,000—the figure was a shrewd choice. And Orthodoxy had no remedy. It was entirely up to him.

Having decided to capitulate, he felt a kind of deadly recklessness. He had never been in the air before. But perhaps it was high time to fly. Everyone had lived enough. And anyway, as the cab crept through the summer lunchtime crowds on Twenty-third Street, there seemed plenty of humankind already.

On the airport bus, he opened his father's copy of the Psalms. The black Hebrew letters only gaped at him like open mouths with tongues hanging down, pointing upward, flaming but dumb. He tried—forcing. It did no good. The tunnel, the swamps, the auto skeletons, machine entrails, dumps, gulls, sketchy Newark trembling in fiery summer, held his attention minutely. As though he were not Isaac Braun but a man who took pictures. Then in the plane running with concentrated fury to take off—the power to pull away from the magnetic earth; and more: When he saw the ground tilt backward, the machine rising from the runway, he said to himself in clear internal words, "*Shema Yisroel*," Hear, O Israel, God alone is God! On the right, New York leaned gigantically seaward, and the plane with a jolt of retracted wheels turned toward the river. The Hudson green within green, and rough with tide and wind. Isaac released the breath he had been holding, but sat belted tight. Above the marvelous bridges, over clouds, sailing in atmosphere, you know better than ever that you are no angel.

The flight was short. From Albany airport, Isaac phoned his bank. He told Spinwall, with whom he did business there, that he needed $20,000 in cash. "No problem," said Spinwall. "We have it."

Isaac explained to Dr. Braun, "I have passbooks for my savings accounts in my safe-deposit box."

Probably in individual accounts of $10,000, protected by federal deposit insurance. He must have had bundles of these.

He went through the round entrance of the vault, the mammoth delicate door, circular, like the approaching moon seen by space navigators. A taxi waited as he drew the money and took him, the dollars in his briefcase, to the hospital. Then at the hospital, the hopeless flesh and melancholy festering and drug odors, the splashy flowers and wrinkled garments. In the large cage elevator that could take in whole beds, pulmotors, and laboratory machines, his eyes were fixed on the silent, beautiful Negro woman dreaming at the control as they moved slowly from lobby to mezzanine, from mezzanine to first. The two were alone, and since there was no going faster, he found himself observing her strong, handsome legs, her bust, the gold wire and glitter of her glasses, and the sensual bulge in her throat, just under the chin. In spite of himself, struck by these as he slowly rose to his sister's deathbed.

At the elevator, as the gate opened, was his brother Mutt.

"Isaac!"

"How is she?"

"Very bad."

"Well, I'm here. With the money."

Confused, Mutt did not know how to face him. He seemed frightened. Tina's power over Mutt had always been great. Though he was three or four years her senior. Isaac somewhat understood what moved him and said, "That's all right, Mutt, if I have to pay. I'm ready. On her terms."

"She may not even know."

"Take it. Say I'm here. I want to see my sister, Mutt."

Unable to look at Isaac, Mutt received the briefcase and went in to Tina. Isaac moved away from her door without glancing through the slot. Because he could not stand still, he moved down the corridor, hands clasped behind his back. Past the rank of empty wheelchairs. Repelled by these things which were made for weakness. He hated such objects, hated the stink of hospitals. He was sixty years old. He knew the route he, too, must go, and soon. But only knew, did not yet feel it. Death still was at a distance. As for handing over the money, about which Mutt was ashamed, taking part unwillingly in something unjust, grotesque— yes, it was farfetched, like things women imagined they wanted in pregnancy, hungry for peaches, or beer, or eating plaster from the walls. But as for himself, as soon as he handed over the money, he felt no more concern for it. It was nothing. He was glad to be rid of it. He could hardly understand this about himself. Once the money was given, the torment stopped. Nothing at all. The thing was done to punish, to characterize him, to convict him of something, to put him in a category. But the effect was just the opposite. What category? Where was it? If she thought it made him suffer, it did not. If she thought she understood his soul better than anyone—his poor dying sister; no, she did not.

And Dr. Braun, feeling with them this work of wit and despair, this last attempt to exchange significance, rose, stood, looking at the shafts of ice, the tatters of vapor in winter blue.

Then Tina's private nurse opened the door and beckoned to Isaac. He hurried in and stopped with a suffocated look. Her upper body was wasted and yellow. Her belly was huge with the growth, and her legs, her ankles were swollen. Her distorted feet had freed themselves from the cover. The soles like clay. The skin was tight on her skull. The hair was white. An intravenous tube was taped to her arm, and other tubes from her body into excretory jars beneath the bed. Mutt had laid the briefcase before her. It had not been unstrapped. Fleshless, hair coarse, and the meaning of her black eyes impossible to understand, she was looking at Isaac.

"Tina!"

"I wondered," she said.

"It's all there."

But she swept the briefcase from her and in a choked voice said, "No. Take it." He went to kiss her. Her free arm was lifted and tried to embrace him. She was too feeble, too drugged. He felt the bones of his obese sister. Death. The end. The grave. They were weeping. And Mutt, turning away at the foot of the bed, his mouth twisted open and the tears running from his eyes. Tina's tears were much thicker and slower.

The ring she had taken from Aunt Rose was tied to Tina's wasted finger with dental floss. She held out her hand to the nurse. It was all prearranged. The nurse cut the thread. Tina said to Isaac, "Not the money. I don't want it. You take Mama's ring."

And Dr. Braun, bitterly moved, tried to grasp what emotions were. What good were they! What were they for! And no one wanted them now. Perhaps the cold eye was better. On life, on death. But, again, the cold of the eye would be proportional to the degree of heat within. But once humankind had grasped its own idea, that it was human and human through such passions, it began to exploit, to play, to disturb for the sake of exciting disturbance, to make an uproar, a crude circus of feelings. So the Brauns wept for Tina's death. Isaac held his mother's ring in his hand. Dr. Braun, too, had tears in his eyes. Oh, these Jews—these Jews! Their feelings, their hearts! Dr. Braun often wanted nothing more than to stop all this. For what came of it? One after another you gave over your dying. One by one they went. You went. Childhood, family, friendship, love were stifled in the grave. And these tears! When you wept them from the heart, you felt you justified something, understood something. But what did you understand? Again, *nothing!* It was only an intimation of understanding. A promise that mankind might—*might*, mind you—eventually, through its gift which might—*might* again!—be a divine gift, comprehend why it lived. Why life, why death.

And again, why these particular forms—these Isaacs and these Tinas? When Dr. Braun closed his eyes, he saw, red on black, something like molecular processes—the only true heraldry of being. As later, in the close black darkness when the short day ended, he went to the dark kitchen window to have a look at stars. These things cast outward by a great begetting spasm billions of years ago.

LOOKING FOR MR. GREEN

Whatsoever thy hand findeth to do, do it with thy might. . . .

Hard work? No, it wasn't really so hard. He wasn't used to walking and stair-climbing, but the physical difficulty of his new job was not what George Grebe felt most. He was delivering relief checks in the Negro district, and although he was a native Chicagoan this was not a part of the city he knew much about—it needed a depression to introduce him to it. No, it wasn't literally hard work, not as reckoned in foot-pounds, but yet he was beginning to feel the strain of it, to grow aware of its peculiar difficulty. He could find the streets and numbers, but the clients were not where they were supposed to be, and he felt like a hunter inexperienced in the camouflage of his game. It was an unfavorable day, too—fall, and cold, dark weather, windy. But, anyway, instead of shells in his deep trenchcoat pocket he had the cardboard of checks, punctured for the spindles of the file, the holes reminding him of the holes in player-piano paper. And he didn't look much like a hunter, either; his was a city figure entirely, belted up in this Irish conspirator's coat. He was slender without being tall, stiff in the back, his legs looking shabby in a pair of old tweed pants gone through and fringy at the cuffs. With this stiffness, he kept his head forward, so that his face was red from the sharpness of the weather; and it was an indoors sort of face with gray eyes that persisted in some kind of thought and yet seemed to avoid definiteness of conclusion. He wore sideburns that surprised you somewhat by the tough curl of the blond hair and the effect of assertion in their length. He was not so mild as he looked, nor so youthful; and nevertheless there was no effort on his part to seem what he was not. He was an educated man; he was a bachelor; he was in some ways simple; without lushing, he liked a drink; his luck had not been good. Nothing was deliberately hidden.

He felt that his luck was better than usual today. When he had reported for work that morning he had expected to be shut up in the relief office at a clerk's job, for he had been hired downtown as a clerk, and he was glad to have, instead, the freedom of the streets and welcomed, at least at first, the vigor of the cold and even the blowing of the hard wind. But on the other hand he was not getting on with the distribution of the checks. It was true that it was a city job; nobody expected you to push too hard at a city job. His supervisor, that young Mr. Raynor, had practically told him that. Still, he wanted to do well at it. For one thing, when he knew how quickly he could deliver a batch of checks, he would know also how much time he could expect to clip for himself. And then, too, the clients would be waiting for their money. That was not the most important consideration, though it certainly mattered to him. No, but he wanted to do well, simply for doing-well's sake, to acquit himself decently of a job because he so rarely had a job to do that required just this sort of energy. Of this peculiar energy he now had a superabundance; once it had started to flow, it flowed all too heavily. And, for the time being anyway, he was balked. He could not find Mr. Green.

So he stood in his big-skirted trenchcoat with a large envelope in his hand and papers showing from his pocket, wondering why people should be so hard to locate who were too feeble or sick to come to the station to collect their own checks. But Raynor had told him that tracking them down was not easy at first and had offered him some advice on how to proceed. "If you can see the postman, he's your first man to ask, and your best bet. If you can't connect with him, try the stores and tradespeople around. Then the janitor and the neighbors. But you'll find the closer you come to your man the less people will tell you. They don't want to tell you anything."

"Because I'm a stranger."

"Because you're white. We ought to have a Negro doing this, but we don't at the moment, and of course you've got to eat, too, and this is public employment. Jobs have to be made. Oh, that holds for me too. Mind you, I'm not letting myself out. I've got three years of seniority on you, that's all. And a law degree. Otherwise, you might be back of the desk and I might be going out into the field this cold day. The same dough pays us both and for the same, exact, identical reason. What's my law degree got to do with it? But you have to pass out these checks, Mr. Grebe, and it'll help if you're stubborn, so I hope you are."

"Yes, I'm fairly stubborn."

Raynor sketched hard with an eraser in the old dirt of his desk, left-handed, and said, "Sure, what else can you answer to such a question. Anyhow, the trouble you're going to have is that they don't like to give information about anybody. They think you're a plain-clothes dick or an installment collector, or summons-server or something like that. Till you've been seen around the neighborhood for a few months and people know you're only from the relief."

It was dark, ground-freezing, pre-Thanksgiving weather;

the wind played hob with the smoke, rushing it down, and Grebe missed his gloves, which he had left in Raynor's office. And no one would admit knowing Green. It was past three o'clock and the postman had made his last delivery. The nearest grocer, himself a Negro, had never heard the name Tulliver Green, or said he hadn't. Grebe was inclined to think that it was true, that he had in the end convinced the man that he wanted only to deliver a check. But he wasn't sure. He needed experience in interpreting looks and signs and, even more, the will not to be put off or denied and even the force to bully if need be. If the grocer did know, he had got rid of him easily. But since most of his trade was with reliefers, why should he prevent the delivery of a check? Maybe Green, or Mrs. Green, if there was a Mrs. Green, patronized another grocer. And was there a Mrs. Green? It was one of Grebe's great handicaps that he hadn't looked at any of the case records. Raynor should have let him read files for a few hours. But he apparently saw no need for that, probably considering the job unimportant. Why prepare systematically to deliver a few checks?

But now it was time to look for the janitor. Grebe took in the building in the wind and gloom of the late November day—trampled, frost-hardened lots on one side; on the other, an automobile junk yard and then the infinite work of Elevated frames, weak-looking, gaping with rubbish fires; two sets of leaning brick porches three stories high and a flight of cement stairs to the cellar. Descending, he entered the underground passage, where he tried the doors until one opened and he found himself in the furnace room. There someone rose toward him and approached, scraping on the coal grit and bending under the canvas-jacketed pipes.

"Are you the janitor?"

"What do you want?"

"I'm looking for a man who's supposed to be living here. Green."

"What Green?"

"Oh, you maybe have more than one Green?" said Grebe with new, pleasant hope. "This is Tulliver Green."

"I don't think I c'n help you, mister. I don't know any."

"A crippled man."

The janitor stood bent before him. Could it be that he was crippled? Oh, God! what if he was. Grebe's gray eyes sought with excited difficulty to see. But no, he was only very short and stooped. A head awakened from meditation, a strong-haired beard, low, wide shoulders. A staleness of sweat and coal rose from his black shirt and the burlap sack he wore as an apron.

"Crippled how?"

Grebe thought and then answered with the light voice of unmixed candor, "I don't know. I've never seen him." This was damaging, but his only other choice was to make a lying guess, and he was not up to it. "I'm delivering checks for the relief to shut-in cases. If he weren't crippled he'd come to collect himself. That's why I said crippled. Bedridden, chair-ridden—is there anybody like that?"

This sort of frankness was one of Grebe's oldest talents, going back to childhood. But it gained him nothing here.

"No suh. I've got four buildin's same as this that I take care of. I don' know all the tenants, leave alone the tenants' tenants. The rooms turn over so fast, people movin' in and out every day. I can't tell you."

The janitor opened his grimy lips but Grebe did not hear him in the piping of the valves and the consuming pull of air to flame in the body of the furnace. He knew, however, what he had said.

"Well, all the same, thanks. Sorry I bothered you. I'll prowl around upstairs again and see if I can turn up someone who knows him."

Once more in the cold air and early darkness he made the short circle from the cellarway to the entrance crowded between the brickwork pillars and began to climb to the third floor. Pieces of plaster ground under his feet; strips of brass tape from which the carpeting had been torn away marked old boundaries at the sides. In the passage, the cold reached him worse than in the street; it touched him to the bone. The hall toilets ran like springs. He thought grimly as he heard the wind burning around the building with a sound like that of the furnace, that this was a great piece of constructed shelter. Then he struck a match in the gloom and searched for names and numbers among the writings and scribbles on the walls. He saw WHOODY-DOODY GO TO JESUS, and zigzags, caricatures, sexual scrawls, and curses. So the sealed rooms of pyramids were also decorated, and the caves of human dawn.

The information on his card was, TULLIVER GREEN— APT 3D. There were no names, however, and no numbers. His shoulders drawn up, tears of cold in his eyes, breathing vapor, he went the length of the corridor and told himself that if he had been lucky enough to have the temperament for it he would bang on one of the doors and bawl out "Tulliver Green!" until he got results. But it wasn't in him to make an uproar and he continued to burn matches, passing the light over the walls. At the rear, in a corner off the hall, he discovered a door he had not seen before and he thought it best to investigate. It sounded empty when he knocked, but a young Negress answered, hardly more than a girl. She opened only a bit, to guard the warmth of the room.

"Yes suh?"

"I'm from the district relief station on Prairie Avenue. I'm looking for a man named Tulliver Green to give him his check. Do you know him?"

No, she didn't; but he thought she had not understood anything of what he had said. She had a dream-bound, dream-blind face, very soft and black, shut off. She wore a man's jacket and pulled the ends together at her throat. Her hair was parted in three directions, at the sides and transversely, standing up at the front in a dull puff.

"Is there somebody around here who might know?"

"I jus' taken this room las' week."

He observed that she shivered, but even her shiver was somnambulistic and there was no sharp consciousness of cold in the big smooth eyes of her handsome face.

"All right, miss, thank you. Thanks," he said, and went to try another place.

Here he was admitted. He was grateful, for the room was warm. It was full of people, and they were silent as he entered—ten people, or a dozen, perhaps more, sitting on benches like a parliament. There was no light, properly speaking, but a tempered darkness that the window gave, and everyone seemed to him enormous, the men padded out in heavy work clothes and winter coats, and the women huge, too, in their sweaters, hats, and old furs. And, besides, bed and bedding, a black cooking range, a piano piled towering to the ceiling with papers, a dining-room table of the old style of prosperous Chicago. Among these people Grebe, with his cold-heightened fresh color and his smaller stature, entered like a schoolboy. Even though he was met with smiles and good will, he knew, before a single word was spoken, that all the currents ran against him and that he would make no headway. Nevertheless he began. "Does anybody here know how I can deliver a check to Mr. Tulliver Green?"

"Green?" It was the man that had let him in who answered. He was in short sleeves, in a checkered shirt, and had a queer, high head, profusely overgrown and long as a shako; the veins entered it strongly from his forehead. "I never heard mention of him. Is this where he live?"

"This is the address they gave me at the station. He's a sick man, and he'll need his check. Can't anybody tell me where to find him?"

He stood his ground and waited for a reply, his crimson wool scarf wound about his neck and drooping outside his trenchcoat, pockets weighted with the block of checks and official forms. They must have realized that he was not a college boy employed afternoons by a bill collector, trying foxily to pass for a relief clerk, recognized that he was an older man who knew himself what need was, who had had more than an average seasoning in hardship. It was evident enough if you looked at the marks under his eyes and at the sides of his mouth.

"Anybody know this sick man?"

"No suh." On all sides he saw heads shaken and smiles of denial. No one knew. And maybe it was true, he considered, standing silent in the earthen, musky human gloom of the place as the rumble continued. But he could never really be sure.

"What's the matter with this man?" said shako-head.

"I've never seen him. All I can tell you is that he can't come in person for his money. It's my first day in this district."

"Maybe they given you the wrong number?"

"I don't believe so. But where else can I ask about him?" He felt that this persistence amused them deeply, and in a way he shared their amusement that he should stand up so tenaciously to them. Though smaller, though slight, he was his own man, he retracted nothing about himself, and he looked back at them, gray-eyed, with amusement and also with a sort of courage. On the bench some man spoke in his throat, the words impossible to catch, and a woman answered with a wild, shrieking laugh, which was quickly cut off.

"Well, so nobody will tell me?"

"Ain't nobody who knows."

"At least, if he lives here, he pays rent to someone. Who manages the building?"

"Greatham Company. That's on Thirty-ninth Street."

Grebe wrote it in his pad. But, in the street again, a sheet of wind-driven paper clinging to his leg while he deliberated what direction to take next, it seemed a feeble lead to follow. Probably this Green didn't rent a flat, but a room. Sometimes there were as many as twenty people in an apartment; the real-estate agent would know only the lessee. And not even the agent could tell you who the renters were. In some places the beds were even used in shifts, watchmen or jitney drivers or short-order cooks in night joints turning out after a day's sleep and surrendering their beds to a sister, a nephew, or perhaps a stranger, just off the bus. There were large numbers of newcomers in this terrific, blight-bitten portion of the city between Cottage Grove and Ashland, wandering from house to house and room to room. When you saw them, how could you know them? They didn't carry bundles on their backs or look picturesque. You only saw a man, a Negro, walking in the street or riding in the car, like everyone else, with his thumb closed on a transfer. And therefore how were you supposed to tell? Grebe thought the Greatham agent would only laugh at his question.

But how much it would have simplified the job to be able to say that Green was old, or blind, or consumptive. An hour in the files, taking a few notes, and he needn't have been at such a disadvantage. When Raynor gave him the block of checks he asked, "How much should I know about these people?" Then Raynor had looked as though he were preparing to accuse him of trying to make the job more important than it was. He smiled, because by then they were on fine terms, but nevertheless he had been getting ready to say something like that when the confusion began in the station over Staika and her children.

Grebe had waited a long time for this job. It came to him through the pull of an old schoolmate in the Corporation Counsel's office, never a close friend, but suddenly sympathetic and interested—pleased to show, moreover, how well he had done, how strongly he was coming on even in these miserable times. Well, he was coming through strongly, along with the Democratic administration itself. Grebe had gone to see him in City Hall, and they had had a counter lunch or beers at least once a month for a year, and finally it had been possible to swing the job. He didn't mind being assigned the lowest clerical grade, nor even being a messenger, though Raynor thought he did.

This Raynor was an original sort of guy and Grebe had taken to him immediately. As was proper on the first day, Grebe had come early, but he waited long, for Raynor was late. At last he darted into his cubicle of an office as though he had just jumped from one of those hurtling huge red Indian Avenue cars. His thin, rough face was wind-stung and he was grinning and saying something breathlessly to himself. In his hat, a small fedora, and his coat, the velvet collar a neat fit about his neck, and his silk muffler that set off the nervous twist of his chin, he swayed and turned himself in his swivel chair, feet leaving the ground; so that he pranced a little as he sat. Meanwhile he took Grebe's measure out of his eyes, eyes of an unusual vertical length and slightly sardonic. So the two men sat for a while, saying nothing, while the supervisor raised his hat from his miscombed hair and put it in his lap. His cold-darkened hands were not clean. A steel beam passed through the little makeshift room, from which machine belts once had hung. The building was an old factory.

"I'm younger than you; I hope you won't find it hard taking orders from me," said Raynor. "But I don't make them up, either. You're how old, about?"

"Thirty-five."

"And you thought you'd be inside doing paper work. But it so happens I have to send you out."

"I don't mind."

"And it's mostly a Negro load we have in this district."

"So I thought it would be."

"Fine. You'll get along. *C'est un bon boulot.* Do you know French?"

"Some."

"I thought you'd be a university man."

"Have you been in France?" said Grebe.

"No, that's the French of the Berlitz School. I've been at it for more than a year, just as I'm sure people have been, all over the world, office boys in China and braves in Tanganyika. In fact, I damn well know it. Such is the attractive power of civilization. It's overrated, but what do you want? *Que voulez-vous?* I get *Le Rire* and all the spicy papers, just like in Tanganyika. It must be mystifying, out there. But my reason is that I'm aiming at the diplomatic service. I have a cousin who's a courier, and the way he describes it is awfully attractive. He rides in the *wagon-lits* and reads books. While we— What did you do before?"

"I sold."

"Where?"

"Canned meat at Stop and Shop. In the basement."

"And before that?"

"Window shades, at Goldblatt's."

"Steady work?"

"No, Thursdays and Saturdays. I also sold shoes."

"You've been a shoe-dog too. Well. And prior to that? Here it is in your folder." He opened the record. "Saint Olaf's College, instructor in classical languages. Fellow, University of Chicago, 1926–27. I've had Latin, too. Let's trade quotations—'*Dum spiro spero.*' "

" '*Da dextram misero.*' "

" '*Alea jacta est.*' "

" '*Excelsior.*' "

Raynor shouted with laughter, and other workers came to look at him over the partition. Grebe also laughed, feeling pleased and easy. The luxury of fun on a nervous morning.

When they were done and no one was watching or listening, Raynor said rather seriously, "What made you study Latin in the first place? Was it for the priesthood?"

"No."

"Just for the hell of it? For the culture? Oh, the things people think they can pull!" He made his cry hilarious and tragic. "I ran my pants off so I could study for the bar, and I've passed the bar, so I get twelve dollars a week more than you as a bonus for having seen life straight and whole. I'll tell you, as a man of culture, that even though nothing looks to be real, and everything stands for something else, and that thing for another thing, and that thing for a still further one—there ain't any comparison between twenty-five and thirty-seven dollars a week, regardless of the last reality. Don't you think that was clear to your Greeks? They were a thoughtful people, but they didn't part with their slaves."

This was a great deal more than Grebe had looked for in his first interview with his supervisor. He was too shy to show all the astonishment he felt. He laughed a little, aroused, and brushed at the sunbeam that covered his head with its dust. "Do you think my mistake was so terrible?"

"Damn right it was terrible, and you know it now that you've had the whip of hard times laid on your back. You should have been preparing yourself for trouble. Your people must have been well off to send you to the university. Stop me, if I'm stepping on your toes. Did your mother pamper you? Did your father give in to you? Were you brought up tenderly, with permission to go and find out what were the last things that everything else stands for while everybody else labored in the fallen world of appearances?"

"Well, no, it wasn't exactly like that." Grebe smiled. *The fallen world of appearances!* no less. But now it was his turn to deliver a surprise. "We weren't rich. My father was the last genuine English butler in Chicago—"

"Are you kidding?"

"Why should I be?"

"In a livery?"

"In livery. Up on the Gold Coast."

"And he wanted you to be educated like a gentleman?"

"He did not. He sent me to the Armour Institute to study chemical engineering. But when he died I changed schools."

He stopped himself, and considered how quickly Raynor had reached him. In no time he had your valise on the table and all your stuff unpacked. And afterward, in the streets, he was still reviewing how far he might have gone, and how much he might have been led to tell if they had not been interrupted by Mrs. Staika's great noise.

But just then a young woman, one of Raynor's workers, ran into the cubicle exclaiming, "Haven't you heard all the fuss?"

"We haven't heard anything."

"It's Staika, giving out with all her might. The reporters are coming. She said she phoned the papers, and you know she did."

"But what is she up to?" said Raynor.

"She brought her wash and she's ironing it here, with our current, because the relief won't pay her electric bill. She has her ironing board set up by the admitting desk, and her kids are with her, all six. They never are in school more than once a week. She's always dragging them around with her because of her reputation."

"I don't want to miss any of this," said Raynor, jumping up. Grebe, as he followed with the secretary, said, "Who is this Staika?"

"They call her the 'Blood Mother of Federal Street.' She's a professional donor at the hospitals. I think they pay ten dollars a pint. Of course it's no joke, but she makes a very big thing out of it and she and the kids are in the papers all the time."

A small crowd, staff and clients divided by a plywood

barrier, stood in the narrow space of the entrance, and Staika was shouting in a gruff, mannish voice, plunging the iron on the board and slamming it on the metal rest.

"My father and mother came in a steerage, and I was born in our house, Robey by Huron. I'm no dirty immigrant. I'm a U.S. citizen. My husband is a gassed veteran from France with lungs weaker'n paper, that hardly can he go to the toilet by himself. These six children of mine, I have to buy the shoes for their feet with my own blood. Even a lousy little white Communion necktie, that's a couple of drops of blood; a little piece of mosquito veil for my Vadja so she won't be ashamed in church for the other girls, they take my blood for it by Goldblatt. That's how I keep goin'. A fine thing if I had to depend on the relief. And there's plenty of people on the rolls—fakes! There's nothin' *they* can't get, that can go and wrap bacon at Swift and Armour any time. They're lookin' for them by the Yards. They never have to be out of work. Only they rather lay in their lousy beds and eat the public's money." She was not afraid, in a predominantly Negro station, to shout this way about Negroes.

Grebe and Raynor worked themselves forward to get a closer view of the woman. She was flaming with anger and with pleasure at herself, broad and huge, a golden-headed woman who wore a cotton cap laced with pink ribbon. She was barelegged and had on black gym shoes, her Hoover apron was open and her great breasts, not much restrained by a man's undershirt, hampered her arms as she worked at the kid's dress on the ironing board. And the children, silent and white, with a kind of locked obstinacy, in sheepskins and lumberjackets, stood behind her. She had captured the station, and the pleasure this gave her was enormous. Yet her grievances were true grievances. She was telling the truth. But she behaved like a liar. The look of her small eyes was hidden, and while she raged she also seemed to be spinning and planning.

"They send me out college case workers in silk pants to talk me out of what I got comin'. Are they better'n me? Who told them? Fire them. Let 'em go and get married, and then you won't have to cut electric from people's budget."

The chief supervisor, Mr. Ewing, couldn't silence her and he stood with folded arms at the head of his staff, bald, bald-headed, saying to his subordinates like the ex-school principal he was, "Pretty soon she'll be tired and go."

"No she won't," said Raynor to Grebe. "She'll get what she wants. She knows more about the relief even then Ewing. She's been on the rolls for years, and she always gets what she wants because she puts on a noisy show. Ewing knows it. He'll give in soon. He's only saving face. If he gets bad publicity, the Commissioner'll have him on the carpet, downtown. She's got him submerged; she'll submerge everybody in time, and that includes nations and governments."

Grebe replied with his characteristic smile, disagreeing completely. Who would take Staika's orders, and what changes could her yelling ever bring about?

No, what Grebe saw in her, the power that made people listen, was that her cry expressed the war of flesh and blood, perhaps turned a little crazy and certainly ugly, on this place and this condition. And at first, when he went out, the spirit of Staika somehow presided over the whole district for him, and it took color from her; he saw her color, in the spotty curb fires, and the fires under the El, the straight alley of flamy gloom. Later, too, when he went into a tavern for a shot of rye, the sweat of beer, association with West Side Polish streets, made him think of her again.

He wiped the corners of his mouth with his muffler, his handkerchief being inconvenient to reach for, and went out again to get on with the delivery of his checks. The air bit cold and hard and a few flakes of snow formed near him. A train struck by and left a quiver in the frames and a bristling icy hiss over the rails.

Crossing the street, he descended a flight of board steps into a basement grocery, setting off a little bell. It was a dark, long store and it caught you with its stinks of smoked meat, soap, dried peaches, and fish. There was a fire wrinkling and flapping in the little stove, and the proprietor was waiting, an Italian with a long, hollow face and stubborn bristles. He kept his hands warm under his apron.

No, he didn't know Green. You knew people but not names. The same man might not have the same name twice. The police didn't know, either, and mostly didn't care. When somebody was shot or knifed they took the body away and didn't look for the murderer. In the first place, nobody would tell them anything. So they made up a name for the coroner and called it quits. And in the second place, they didn't give a goddamn anyhow. But they couldn't get to the bottom of a thing even if they wanted to. Nobody would get to know even a tenth of what went on among these people. They stabbed and stole, they did every crime and abomination you ever heard of, men and men, women and women, parents and children, worse than the animals. They carried on their own way, and the horrors passed off like a smoke. There was never anything like it in the history of the whole world.

It was a long speech, deepening with every word in its fantasy and passion and becoming increasingly senseless and terrible: a swarm amassed by suggestion and invention, a huge, hugging, despairing knot, a human wheel of heads, legs, bellies, arms, rolling through his shop.

Grebe felt that he must interrupt him. He said sharply, "What are you talking about! All I asked was whether you knew this man."

"That isn't even the half of it. I been here six years. You probably don't want to believe this. But suppose it's true?"

"All the same," said Grebe, "there must be a way to find a person."

The Italian's close-spaced eyes had been queerly concentrated, as were his muscles, while he leaned across the counter trying to convince Grebe. Now he gave up the effort and sat down on his stool. "Oh—I suppose. Once in a while. But I been telling you, even the cops don't get any-where."

"They're always after somebody. It's not the same thing."

"Well, keep trying if you want. I can't help you."

But he didn't keep trying. He had no more time to spend on Green. He slipped Green's check to the back of the block. The next name on the list was FIELD, WINSTON.

He found the back-yard bungalow without the least trou-ble; it shared a lot with another house, a few feet of yard between. Grebe knew these two-shack arrangements. They had been built in vast numbers in the days before the swamps were filled and the streets raised, and they were all the same—a boardwalk along the fence, well under street level, three or four ball-headed posts for clotheslines, greening wood, dead shingles, and a long, long flight of stairs to the rear door.

A twelve-year-old boy let him into the kitchen, and there the old man was, sitting by the table in a wheel chair.

"Oh, it's d' Government man," he said to the boy when Grebe drew out his checks. "Go bring me my box of papers." He cleared a space on the table.

"Oh, you don't have to go to all that trouble," said Grebe. But Field laid out his papers: Social Security card, relief certification, letters from the state hospital in Manteno, and a naval discharge dated San Diego, 1920.

"That's plenty," Grebe said. "Just sign."

"You got to know who I am," the old man said. "You're from the Government. It's not your check, it's a Govern-ment check and you got no business to hand it over till everything is proved."

He loved the ceremony of it, and Grebe made no more objections. Field emptied his box and finished out the circle of cards and letters.

"There's everything I done and been. Just the death certificate and they can close book on me." He said this with a certain happy pride and magnificence. Still he did not sign; he merely held the little pen upright on the golden-green corduroy of his thigh. Grebe did not hurry him. He felt the old man's hunger for conversation.

"I got to get better coal," he said. "I send my little gran'son to the yard with my order and they fill his wagon with screening. The stove ain't made for it. It fall through the grate. The order says Franklin County egg-size coal."

"I'll report it and see what can be done."

"Nothing can be done, I expect. You know and I know. There ain't no little ways to make things better, and the only big thing is money. That's the only sunbeams, money. Nothing is black where it shines, and the only place you see black is where it ain't shining. What we colored have to have is our own rich. There ain't no other way."

Grebe sat, his reddened forehead bridged levelly by his close-cut hair and his cheeks lowered in the wings of his collar—the caked fire shone hard within the isinglass-and-iron frames but the room was not comfortable—sat and listened while the old man unfolded his scheme. This was to create one Negro millionaire a month by subscription. One clever, good-hearted young fellow elected every month would sign a contract to use the money to start a business employing Negroes. This would be advertised by chain letters and word of mouth, and every Negro wage earner would contribute a dollar a month. Within five years there would be sixty millionaires.

"That'll fetch respect," he said with a throat-stopped sound that came out like a foreign syllable. "You got to take and organize all the money that gets thrown away on the policy wheel and horse race. As long as they can take it away from you, they got no respect for you. Money, that's d' sun of human kind!" Field was a Negro of mixed blood, perhaps Cherokee, or Natchez; his skin was reddish. And he sounded, speaking about a golden sun in this dark room, and looked, shaggy and slab-headed, with the mingled blood of his face and broad lips, the little pen still upright in his hand, like one of the underground kings of mythology, old judge Minos himself.

And now he accepted the check and signed. Not to soil the slip, he held it down with his knuckles. The table budged and creaked, the center of the gloomy, heathen midden of the kitchen covered with bread, meat, and cans, and the scramble of papers.

"Don't you think my scheme'd work?"

"It's worth thinking about. Something ought to be done, I agree."

"It'll work if people will do it. That's all. That's the only thing, any time. When they understand it in the same way, all of them."

"That's true," said Grebe, rising. His glance met the old man's.

"I know you got to go," he said. "Well, God bless you, boy, you ain't been sly with me. I can tell it in a minute."

He went back through the buried yard. Someone nursed a candle in a shed, where a man unloaded kindling wood from a sprawl-wheeled baby buggy and two voices carried on a high conversation. As he came up the sheltered passage he heard the hard boost of the wind in the branches and against the house fronts, and then, reaching the sidewalk, he saw the needle-eye red of cable towers in the open icy height hundreds of feet above the river and the factories—those keen points. From here, his view was obstructed all the way to the South Branch and its timber banks, and the cranes beside the water. Rebuilt after the Great Fire, this part of the city was, not fifty years later, in ruins again, factories boarded up, buildings deserted or fallen, gaps of prairie between. But it wasn't desolation that this made you feel, but rather a faltering of organization that set free a huge energy, an escaped, unattached, unregulated power from the giant raw place. Not only must people feel it but, it seemed to Grebe, they were compelled to match it. In their very bodies. He no less than others, he realized. Say that his parents had been servants in their time, whereas he was not supposed to be one. He thought that they had never done any service like this, which no one visible asked for, and probably flesh and blood could not even perform. Nor could anyone show why it should be performed; or see where the performance would lead. That did not mean that he wanted to be released from it, he realized with a grimly pensive face. On the contrary. He had something to do. To be compelled to feel this energy and yet have no task to do—that was horrible; that was suffering; he knew what that was. It was now quitting time. Six o'clock. He could go home if he liked, to his room, that is, to wash in hot water, to pour a drink, lie down on his quilt, read the paper, eat some liver paste on crackers before going out to dinner. But to think of this actually made him feel a little sick, as though he had swallowed hard air. He had six checks left, and he was determined to deliver at least one of these: Mr. Green's check.

So he started again. He had four or five dark blocks to go, past open lots, condemned houses, old foundations, closed schools, black churches, mounds, and he reflected that there must be many people alive who had once seen the neighborhood rebuilt and new. Now there was a second layer of ruins; centuries of history accomplished through human massing. Numbers had given the place forced growth; enormous numbers had also broken it down. Objects once so new, so concrete that it could never have occurred to anyone they stood for other things, had crumbled. Therefore, reflected Grebe, the secret of them was out. It was that they stood for themselves by agreement, and were natural and not unnatural by agreement, and when the things themselves collapsed the agreement became visible. What was it, otherwise, that kept cities from looking peculiar?

Rome, that was almost permanent, did not give rise to thoughts like these. And was it abidingly real? But in Chicago, where the cycles were so fast and the familiar died out, and again rose changed, and died again in thirty years, you saw the common agreement or covenant, and you were forced to think about appearances and realities. (He remembered Raynor and he smiled. Raynor was a clever boy.) Once you had grasped this, a great many things became intelligible. For instance, why Mr. Field should conceive such a scheme. Of course, if people were to agree to create a millionaire, a real millionaire would come into existence. And if you wanted to know how Mr. Field was inspired to think of this, why, he had within sight of his kitchen window the chart, the very bones of a successful scheme—the El with its blue and green confetti of signals. People consented to pay dimes and ride the crash-box cars, and so it was a success. Yet how absurd it looked; how little reality there was to start with. And yet Yerkes, the great financier who built it, had known that he could get people to agree to do it. Viewed as itself, what a scheme of a scheme it seemed, how close to an appearance. Then why wonder at Mr. Field's idea? He had grasped a principle. And then Grebe remembered, too, that Mr. Yerkes had established the Yerkes Observatory and endowed it with millions. Now how did the notion come to him in his New York museum of a palace or his Aegean-bound yacht to give money to astronomers? Was he awed by the success of his bizarre enterprise and therefore ready to spend money to find out where in the universe being and seeming were identical? Yes, he wanted to know what abides; and whether flesh is Bible grass; and he offered money to be burned in the fire of suns. Okay, then, Grebe thought further, these things exist because people consent to exist with them—we have got so far—and also there is a reality which doesn't depend on consent but within which consent is a game. But what about need, the need that keeps so many vast thousands in position? You tell me that, you *private* little gentleman and *decent* soul—he used these words against himself scornfully. Why is the consent given to misery? And why so painfully ugly? Because there is *something* that is dismal and permanently ugly? Here he sighed and gave it up, and thought it was enough for the present moment that he had a real check in his pocket for a Mr. Green who must be real beyond question. If only his neighbors didn't think they had to conceal him.

This time he stopped at the second floor. He struck a match and found a door. Presently a man answered his knock and Grebe had the check ready and showed it even before he began. "Does Tulliver Green live here? I'm from the relief."

The man narrowed the opening and spoke to someone at his back.

"Does he live here?"

"Uh-uh. No."

"Or anywhere in this building? He's a sick man and he can't come for his dough." He exhibited the check in the light, which was smoky—the air smelled of charred lard— and the man held off the brim of his cap to study it.

"Uh-uh. Never seen the name."

"There's nobody around here that uses crutches?"

He seemed to think, but it was Grebe's impression that he was simply waiting for a decent interval to pass.

"No, suh. Nobody I ever see."

"I've been looking for this man all afternoon"—Grebe spoke out with sudden force—"and I'm going to have to carry this check back to the station. It seems strange not to be able to find a person to *give* him something when you're looking for him for a good reason. I suppose if I had bad news for him I'd find him quick enough."

There was a responsive motion in the other man's face. "That's right, I reckon."

"It almost doesn't do any good to have a name if you

can't be found by it. It doesn't stand for anything. He might as well not have any," he went on, smiling. It was as much of a concession as he could make to his desire to laugh.

"Well, now, there's a little old knot-back man I see once in a while. He might be the one you lookin' for. Downstairs."

"Where? Right side or left? Which door?"

"I don't know which. Thin-face little knot-back with a stick."

But no one answered at any of the doors on the first floor. He went to the end of the corridor, searching by matchlight, and found only a stairless exit to the yard, a drop of about six feet. But there was a bungalow near the alley, an old house like Mr. Field's. To jump was unsafe. He ran from the front door, through the underground passage and into the yard. The place was occupied. There was a light through the curtains, upstairs. The name on the ticket under the broken, scoop-shaped mailbox was Green! He exultantly rang the bell and pressed against the locked door. Then the lock clicked faintly and a long staircase opened before him. Someone was slowly coming down—a woman. He had the impression in the weak light that she was shaping her hair as she came, making herself presentable, for he saw her arms raised. But it was for support that they were raised; she was feeling her way downward, down the wall, stumbling. Next he wondered about the pressure of her feet on the treads; she did not seem to be wearing shoes. And it was a freezing stairway. His ring had got her out of bed, perhaps, and she had forgotten to put them on. And then he saw that she was not only shoeless but naked; she was entirely naked, climbing down while she talked to herself, a heavy woman, naked and drunk. She blundered into him. The contact of her breasts, though they touched only his coat, made him go back against the door with a blind shock. See what he had tracked down, in his hunting game!

The woman was saying to herself, furious with insult, "So I cain't fuck, huh? I'll show that son of a bitch kin I, cain't I."

What should he do now? Grebe asked himself. Why, he should go. He should turn away and go. He couldn't talk to this woman. He couldn't keep her standing naked in the cold. But when he tried he found himself unable to turn away.

He said, "Is this where Mr. Green lives?"

But she was still talking to herself and did not hear him.

"Is this Mr. Green's house?"

At last she turned her furious drunken glance on him. "What do you want?"

Again her eyes wandered from him; there was a dot of blood in their enraged brilliance. He wondered why she didn't feel the cold.

"I'm from the relief."

"Awright, what?"

"I've got a check for Tulliver Green."

This time she heard him and put out her hand.

"No, no, for *Mr.* Green. He's got to sign," he said. How was he going to get Green's signature tonight!

"I'll take it. He cain't."

He desperately shook his head, thinking of Mr. Field's precautions about identification. "I can't let you have it. It's for him. Are you Mrs. Green?"

"Maybe I is, and maybe I ain't. Who want to know?"

"Is he upstairs?"

"Awright. Take it up yourself, you goddamn fool."

Sure, he was a goddamn fool. Of course he could not go up because Green would probably be drunk and naked, too. And perhaps he would appear on the landing soon. He looked eagerly upward. Under the light was a high narrow brown wall. Empty! It remained empty!

"Hell with you, then!" he heard her cry. To deliver a check for coal and clothes, he was keeping her in the cold.

She did not feel it, but his face was burning with frost and self-ridicule. He backed away from her

"I'll come tomorrow, tell him."

"Ah, hell with you. Don' never come. What you doin' here in the nighttime? Don' come back." She yelled so that he saw the breadth of her tongue. She stood astride in the long cold box of the hall and held on to the banister and the wall. The bungalow itself was shaped something like a box, a clumsy, high box pointing into the freezing air with its sharp, wintry lights.

"If you are Mrs. Green, I'll give you the check," he said, changing his mind.

"Give here, then." She took it, took the pen offered with it in her left hand, and tried to sign the receipt on the wall. He looked around, almost as though to see whether his madness was being observed, and came near believing that someone was standing on a mountain of used tires in the auto-junking shop next door.

"But are you Mrs. Green?" he now thought to ask. But she was already climbing the stairs with the check, and it was too late, if he had made an error, if he was now in trouble, to undo the thing. But he wasn't going to worry about it. Though she might not be Mrs. Green, he was convinced that Mr. Green was upstairs. Whoever she was, the woman stood for Green, whom he was not to see this time. Well, you silly bastard, he said to himself, so you think you found him. So what? Maybe you really did find him—what of it? But it was important that there was a real Mr. Green whom they could not keep him from reaching because he seemed to come as an emissary from hostile appearances. And though the self-ridicule was slow to diminish, and his face still blazed with it, he had, nevertheless, a feeling of elation, too. "For after all," he said, "he *could* be found!"

THE GONZAGA MANUSCRIPTS

Buttoned to the throat in a long, soft overcoat, dark green, Clarence Feiler got off the Hendaye Express in the Madrid station. It was late afternoon and it was raining, and the station with its throng and its dim orange lights seemed sunken under darkness and noise. The gaunt horselike Spanish locomotives screamed off their steam and the hurrying passengers struggled in the narrow gates. Porters and touts approached Clarence, obviously a foreigner, judging by his small blond beard, blue eyes, almost brimless hat, long coat, and crepe-soled shoes. But he carried his own bag and had no need of them. This was not his first visit to Madrid. An old limousine took him to the Pensión La Granja, where he had a room reserved. This limousine probably had run on the boulevards of Madrid before Clarence was born but it was mechanically still beautiful. In the spacious darkness of the back seat the windows were like the glass of an old cabinet, and he listened happily to the voice of the wonderful old motor. Where could you get another ride like this, on such an evening, through such a place? Clarence loved Spanish cities, even the poorest and barrenest, and the capitals stirred his heart as no other places did. He had first come as an undergraduate, a mere kid, studying Spanish literature at the University of Minnesota; and then he had come again and seen the ruins of the Civil War. This time he came not as a tourist but on a quest. He had heard from a Spanish Republican refugee in California, where he now lived, that there were more than a hundred poems by Manuel Gonzaga somewhere in Madrid. Not a single Spanish publishing house could print them because they were so critical of the Army and the State. It was hard to believe that poems by one of the greatest of modern Spanish geniuses could be suppressed, but the refugee gave Clarence reliable proof that it was so. He showed him letters to one of Gonzaga's nephews from a man named Guzmán del Nido, Gonzaga's friend and literary executor, with whom he had served in North Africa, admitting that he had once had the poems but had given them up to a certain Countess del Camino since most of them were love poems addressed to her. The countess had died during the war, her home had been looted, and he didn't know what had become of the poems.

"Perhaps Guzmán doesn't care, either," said the refugee. "He's one of these people who think everything has come to an end anyway, and they might as well live comfortably. Guzmán del Nido lives very comfortably. He's rich. He is a member of the Cortes."

"Money doesn't have to do that to you," said Clarence, who had a little money himself. He was not exactly a rich man, but he didn't have to work for a living. "He must have a bad character not to care about his friend's work. And such work! You know, I was just killing time in graduate school till I came across Gonzaga. The year I spent doing my thesis on *Los Huesos Secos* was the first good year I had

had since I was a boy. There hasn't been anything like it since. I'm not much on modern poetry in English. Some of it is very fine, of course, but it doesn't express much wish to live. To live as a creature, that is. As if it were not good enough. But the first time I opened Gonzaga I read:

> These few bits of calcium my teeth are,
> And these few ohms my brain is,
> May make you think I am nothing but puny.
> Let me tell you, sir,
> I am like any creature—
> A creature.

I felt right away and in spite of this ironical turn that I was in touch with a poet who could show me how to go on, and what attitude to take toward life. The great, passionate poems carried me away, like 'The Poem of Night,' which I still know by heart from beginning to end and which often seems like the only thing I really have got—" Clarence was sometimes given to exaggeration. "Or take the poem called 'Confession,' the one that goes:

> I used to welcome all
> And now I fear all.
> If it rained it was comforting
> And if it shone, comforting,
> But now my very weight is dreadful. . . .

When I read that, Gonzaga made me understand how we lose everything by trying to become everything. This was the most valuable lesson of my life, I think. Gosh! There should be someone trying to find those posthumous poems. They ought not to be given up. They must be marvelous."

He felt, suddenly, as if he had been thrown into a race, terribly excited, full of effort, feverish—and profoundly grateful. For Clarence had not found his occupation and had nothing to do. He did not think it right to marry until he had found something and could offer a wife leadership.

His beard was grown not to hide weaknesses but as a project, to give his life shape. He was becoming an eccentric; it was all he could do with his good impulses. As yet he did not realize that these impulses were religious. He was too timid to say he believed in God, and he couldn't think that it would matter to anyone what he believed. Since he was weak, it would be said, he must have some such belief. However, he was really enthusiastic about Gonzaga, and to recover this inspired Spaniard's poems was something that mattered. And "Does it really matter?" was always the test question. It filled Clarence with secret pleasure to know that he was not indifferent, at bottom pretending. It *did* matter, and what mattered might save him. He was in Madrid not to perform an act of cultural piety but to do a decent and necessary thing, namely, bring the testimony of a great man before the world. Which certainly could use it.

As soon as he arrived at the Pensión La Granja and the lamps were lit in his room, a comfortable large room with balconies facing the trees of the Retiro, Madrid's biggest park, Clarence called for the porter and sent off two letters. One was addressed to Guzmán del Nido, Gonzaga's comrade-in-arms of the Moroccan War and literary executor, and the other to a Miss Faith Ungar on García de Paredes Street. This Miss Ungar was an art student, or rather student of art history; her fiancé was an airline pilot who brought in cheaper pesetas from Tangiers. Clarence disliked black-marketing, but the legal rate of exchange was ridiculous; he was prepared to pay a lot of money for those manuscripts and at eighteen to one he might spend a small fortune.

His landlady came to welcome him to the *pensión*—a pale big woman with a sort of turban of hair wound spirally to a point. She came also to collect his passport and other travel papers for police inspection and to give him a briefing on her guests. A retired general was the oldest. She had also some people from British Shell and the widow of a

Minister and six members of a Brazilian trade delegation, so the dining room was full. "And are you a tourist?" she said, glancing at the *tríptico*, the elaborate police document all travelers have to carry in Spain.

"In a way," said Clarence, guardedly. He didn't like to be thought of as a tourist, and yet secrecy was necessary. Gonzaga's poems, though unpublished, would probably come under the head of national treasure.

"Or have you come to study something?"

"Yes, that's it."

"There's a great deal here to interest people from a country as new as yours."

"There certainly is," he said, his rosy beard-lengthened face turned to her, seeming perfectly sincere. The color of his mouth was especially vivid in the lamplight. It was not yet full evening and the rain was stopping. Beyond the trees of the Retiro the sky was making itself clear of clouds, and a last yellow daylight pierced the water-gray. Trolley sparks scratched green sparks within the locust trees.

A bell rang, an old hand bell, announcing dinner. A maid passed, ringing it proudly, her shoulders thrown back.

The guests were eating soup in the dining room, an interior room, not very airy, with dark red, cloth-covered walls. The Brazilians were having a lively conversation. The old general, feeble-headed, eyes nearly extinct, was bothering the soup with his spoon but not eating. Doña Elvia seated Clarence with a hefty British lady. He knew he must expect to have trouble with her. She was in a bad way. Her face was heavily made up; she thought she was a person of charm, and she did have a certain charm, but her eyes were burning. Tresses of dark-reddish hair fought strongly for position on her head.

"If you came here with the intention of having fun, you won't have it in Madrid. I've been here twenty years and never had any," she said. "By now I'm so tired out I don't even look for any. I don't read any books, I don't go to the cinema, and I can just barely stand to read *Coyote* and look at the funnies. I can't understand why so many Americans want to come here. They're all over the place. One of your bishops was arrested at Santander for bathing without the top of his costume."

"Really?"

"They're very strict in Spain about dress. I suppose if they had known he was a bishop they would have let him alone. However, in the water . . ."

"It's strange," said Clarence. "Well, anyway, he's not one of *my* bishops. I have no bishops."

"You do have Congressmen, though. Two of those had their pants stolen while taking a nap on the Barcelona Express. They had hung their pants up because of the heat. The thieves reached into the compartment from the roof and pinched them. It happened in broad daylight. They carried about two thousand dollars each. Don't they have wallets? Why do they carry so much money in their pockets?"

Clarence frowned. "Yes, I read about that," he said. "I can't tell you why they carry so much money in their trouser pockets. Maybe that's the custom down South. It's none of my business, though."

"I'm afraid I'm annoying you," she said. She was not afraid at all; a bold look of enjoyment had entered her eyes. She was trying to bait him. Why? he wondered; he found no ready answer.

"You're not annoying me."

"If I am," she said, "it's not absolutely my fault. You know Stendhal once wrote there was a secret principle of unhappiness in the English."

"Is that so?" he said. He looked at her with greater interest. What a busted-up face; full of unhappy vigor and directionless intelligence. Yes, she was astonishing. He felt sorry for her and yet lucky to have met her, in spite of everything.

"Stendhal may have been right. You see, I used to read widely once. I was a cultivated person. But the reason for it was sex, and that went."

"Oh, come, I wouldn't say—"

"I shouldn't be talking like this. It's partly the weather. It's been raining so hard. It isn't supposed to rain like this in the summer. I've never seen so much damned rain. You people may be to blame for that."

"*Who* people? Which people?"

"It could be because of the atom bomb," she said. "The weather has never been normal since the atom thing started. Nobody can tell what this radioactive stuff is doing. Perhaps it's the beginning of the end."

"You make me feel very strange," said Clarence. "But why are the American bombs the dangerous ones? There are others."

"Because one always reads of the Americans exploding them. They do it under water. Holes are torn in the ocean bottom. The cold water rushes in and cools the core of the earth. Then the earth's surface shrinks. No one can tell what will happen. It's affected the weather already."

Clarence's color grew very high and he looked dazed. He paid no attention to his broiled meat and French fried potatoes. "I don't keep up much with science," he said. "I remember I did read somewhere that industry gives off six billion tons of carbon dioxide every year and so the earth is growing warmer because the carbon dioxide in the air is opaque to heat radiation. All that means that the glaciers won't be coming back."

"Yes, but what about Carbon Fourteen? You Americans are filling the air with Carbon Fourteen, which is very dangerous."

"I don't know about it. I am not all Americans. You are

not all the English. You didn't lick the Armada, I didn't open the West. You are not Winston Churchill and I am not the Pentagon."

"I believe you are some sort of fanatic," she announced.

"And I believe you're a nasty old bag!" he said, enraged. He left the table and went to his room.

Half an hour later she knocked at his door. "I'm terribly sorry," she said. "I suppose I did go too far. But it's all right, we're friends now, aren't we? It does you so much good to be angry. It really is good." She did, now, look very friendly and happy.

"It's all right. I'm sorry too," he said.

After all, how would feuding with this Englishwoman help him with his quest? And probably there were wrong ways and right ways of going about it. Gonzaga's poems should be recovered in the spirit of Gonzaga himself. Otherwise, what was the use?

Considering it all in his head, he saw that this Miss Walsh, the Englishwoman, had done him a service by baiting him. Unwittingly, she offered a test of his motive. He could not come to Spain and act badly, blindly. So he was deepened in his thought and in his purpose, and felt an increased debt to Gonzaga and to those poems.

He was in a hurry next morning to get to a bookshop and see what Gonzaga items there were in print. Impatiently he turned himself out of the comfortable bed, pulled on his underpants, dealt nervously with his cuff buttons, washed at his little sink with the glass shelves and pointed faucets, and combed his hair and whiskers with his palms. Odors of soil and flowers came from the Retiro across the freshly watered street. The morning was clear, still, and blue. He took one bite of the brick bits of toast the maid brought, sipped from the immense cup of bitter *café au lait*, and then rushed out to find a bookstore.

At Bucholz's he found only a single volume he had not seen before, a collection of letters from Gonzaga to his father. The frontispiece showed Gonzaga in his lieutenant's uniform—a small man, by Clarence's standard—sitting up straight at the keyboard of an old-fashioned piano, his large eyes opened directly into the camera. Underneath he had noted, "Whenever I am lucky enough to come upon a piano in one of these Moroccan towns, I can, after playing for ten or fifteen minutes, discover how I really feel. Otherwise I am ignorant." Clarence's face colored with satisfaction as he stooped and looked. What a man this Gonzaga was—what a personality! On the very first page was an early version of a poem he had always admired, the one that began:

> Let me hear a sound
> Truly not my own;
> The voice of another,
> Truly other. . . .

The book engrossed him entirely until eleven o'clock. With a sort of hungry emotion, he sat at a café table and read it from cover to cover. It was beautiful. He thanked God for having sent the Republican refugee who had given him the idea of coming to Spain.

Reluctantly he left the café and took a cab to García de Paredes Street, where Miss Ungar lived. He hated to do it, but he needed pesetas, and it was unavoidable.

Again he was lucky. She was not at all the kind of person you would have expected a black-marketing art student to be; she was young and unusually attractive with a long, intelligent white face. Her hair was drawn tightly back over her elongated head and tied off in an arched, sparkling tail. Her eyes were extremely clear. Clarence was greatly taken with her. Even the fact that her teeth, because of the contrast with her very fair skin, were not too bright, impressed him. It proved to him that she was genuine. On a ribbon round her neck she wore a large silver medal.

"Is that a religious thing you're wearing?"

"No. Do you want to look at it?" She bent forward so that it swung free. He picked up the warm piece of silver and read: HELENA WAITE AWARD FOR HISTORICAL STUDIES.

"You won it?"

"Yes."

"Then why are you in this kind of business?"

"And what did you come here for?" she said.

"I need pesetas."

"And we need dollars. My fiancé and I want to buy a house."

"I see."

"Besides, it's a way of meeting a lot of people. You'd be surprised how few interesting people an American woman in Madrid can meet. I can't spend all my time in the Prado or at the Library. The embassy people are about as interesting as a plate of cold-cuts. My fiancé only gets here twice a month. Are you on a holiday?"

"Sort of."

She didn't believe him. She knew he had come with a definite purpose. He could not say why, but this pleased him.

"How do you like the Granja?"

"It's all right. An Englishwoman there lammed into me last night, first about the atom bomb and then saying that I must be a fanatic. She thought I was peculiar."

"Everybody has to make it as he can," she said.

"That's exactly the way I feel about it."

He had thought that the kind of woman who became engaged to an airline pilot might look down on him. She didn't, not in the least. Soon he was wondering how that sort of man could interest her.

"If you have no other plans, why don't you come to lunch with me," he said, "and save me from that Miss Walsh?"

They went out to eat. Though the day had grown hot, she stopped in the courtyard to put on a pair of net gloves; women without gloves were considered common in Madrid.

For his part Clarence thought the momentary grasp of her fingers as she worked them into the gloves was wonderful; what a lot of life she had! Her white face gave off a pleasant heat. As they walked, she told him she couldn't give him many pesetas just yet; she'd pay whatever rate was quoted in the *Tribune* on the day the money arrived. That day, Clarence reflected, would also be the day on which her pilot arrived; he had no business to be disturbed by that, and yet it did disturb him.

Near the Naval Ministry they were stopped by a procession. Priests with banners led it, and after them came a statue of the Virgin carried by four men. A group of barefooted widows followed in their mourning with black mantillas. Old women passed, carrying tapers. Most of these appeared to be old maids, and the flames made a clear additional light near each face. A band played Beethoven's Funeral March. Above the walls of the ministry trees shot their leaves; there was the same odor of flowers and soil that Clarence had smelled that morning, of graves, of summer pines. Across the square, on the car tracks, a welding arc hummed and scalded. The dazzling mouths of tubas and trombones passed by and the lighted tapers moved off into daylight, but it was the bare white feet of the widows treading on dusty asphalt that Clarence watched, and when they were gone he said to Miss Ungar, "Wasn't that splendid? I'm glad I'm here."

His brows had risen; his face was so lively that Miss Ungar laughed and said, "You take it big. I like the way you take it. You ought to be sure to visit Toledo. Have you ever been there?"

"No."

"I go often. I'm doing a study. Come with me next time. I can show you lots of things there."

"There's nothing I'd like better. When do you go again?"

"Tomorrow."

He was disappointed. "Oh, I'm sorry, I can't make it tomorrow," he said. "I arrived yesterday and I'm going to be very busy for a while. Just give me a raincheck, will you? I'll hold you to this. But there is something special I came to do—you guessed that, I suppose—and I can't take the time to go anywhere now. I'm all keyed up."

"Is this mission of yours a secret?"

"In a way. There's an illegal side to it, probably. But I don't think you'd tell on me, and I'm so full of it I'm willing to talk. Have you ever heard of a poet named Gonzaga?"

"Gonzaga? I must have. But I don't think I ever read him."

"You should. He was very great, one of the most original of modern Spanish poets, and in the class of Juan Ramón Jiménez, Lorca, and Machado. I studied him at school and he means a lot to me. To understand what he did, you have to think first of modern literature as a sort of grand council considering what mankind should do next, how we should fill our mortal time, what we should feel, what we should see, where we should get our courage, how we should love or hate, how we should be pure or great or terrible, evil (you know!), and all the rest. This advice of literature has never done much good. But you see God doesn't rule over men as he used to, and for a long time people haven't been able to feel that life was firmly attached at both ends so that they could stand confidently in the middle. That kind of faith is missing, and for many years poets have tried to supply a substitute. Like 'the unacknowledged legislators' or 'the best is yet to be,' or Walt Whitman saying that whoever touched him could be sure he was touching a man. Some have stood up for beauty, and some have stood up for perfect proportion, and the very best have soon gotten tired of art for its own sake. Some took it as their duty to behave like brave performers who try to hold down panic during a theater fire. Very great ones have quit, like Tolstoy, who became a reformer, or like Rimbaud, who went to Abyssinia, and at the end of his life was begging of a priest, *'Montrez-moi. Mon-*

trez . . . Show me something.' Frightening, the lives some of these geniuses led. Maybe they assumed too much responsibility. They knew that if by their poems and novels *they* were fixing values, there must be something wrong with the values. No one man can furnish them. Oh, he may try, if his inspiration is for values, but not if his inspiration is for words. If you throw the full responsibility for meaning and for the establishing of good and evil on poets, they are bound to go down. However, the poets reflected what was happening to everyone. There are people who feel that they are responsible for *everything*. Gonzaga is free from this, and that's why I love him. Here. See what he says in some of these letters. I found this marvelous collection this morning."

His long hands shaking, he pressed flat the little book on the table of the restaurant. Miss Ungar's quiet face expressed more than intellectual interest. "Listen. He writes to his father: 'Many feel they must say it all, whereas all has been said, unsaid, resaid so many times that we are bound to feel futile unless we understand that we are merely adding our voices. Adding them when moved by the spirit. Then and then only.' Or this: 'A poem may outlive its subject—say, my poem about the girl who sang songs on the train—but the poet has no right to expect this. The poem has no greater privilege than the girl.' You see what kind of man he was?"

"Impressive—really!" she said. "I see that."

"I've come to Spain to find some of his unpublished poems. I have some money, and I've never really been able to find the thing that I wanted to do. I'm not original myself, except in some minor way. Anyhow, that's why I'm here. Lots of people call themselves leaders, healers, priests, and spokesmen for God, prophets or witnesses, but Gonzaga was a human being who spoke only as a human being; there was nothing spurious about him. He tried never to misrepresent; he wanted to see. To move you he didn't have to do anything, he merely had to be. We've made the most natural things the hardest of all. Unfortunately for us all, he was killed while still young. But he left some poems to a certain Countess del Camino, and I'm here to locate them."

"It's a grand thing. I wish you luck. I hope people will help."

"Why shouldn't they?"

"I don't know, but don't you expect to run into trouble?"

"Do you think I ought to expect to?"

"If you want my honest opinion, yes."

"I may get the poems—why, just like that," he said. "You never can tell."

"Started, by God!" he said when he received an answer from Guzmán del Nido. The member of the Cortes invited him to dinner. All that day he was in a state, and the weather was peculiarly thick, first glaring sunshine, then explosive rains. "See what I told you," said Miss Walsh. But when Clarence went out late in the afternoon, the sky was clear and pale again and the Palm Sunday leaves braided in the ironwork of balconies were withering in the sunlight. He walked to the Puerta del Sol with its crowd of pleasure-seekers, beggars, curb-haunters, wealthy women, soldiers, cops, lottery-ticket and fountain-pen peddlers, and priests, humble door-openers, chair-menders, and musicians. At seven-thirty he boarded a streetcar, following directions; it seemed to take him to every other point of the city first. Finally, with his transfer, the wisp of trolley paper still in his hand, he got off and mounted a bare stony alley at the top of which was the del Nido villa. Suddenly there was another cloudburst—*una tormenta* was what the Madrileños called it. No doorway offered cover and he was drenched. At the gate he had to wait a long while for the porter to answer his ring, perhaps five minutes in the hard rain. This would probably give comfort to the Englishwoman with her atomic theories. His nervous eyes seemed to catch some of the slaty blue of the pouring rain cloud; his blond beard darkened, and he pulled in his shoulders. The tall gate opened. The porter held out an umbrella in his brown fist. Clarence walked past him. Too late for umbrellas. The rain stopped when he was halfway up the path.

So he was at a disadvantage when Guzmán del Nido came forward to meet him. He walked clumsily in his sodden wool suit. It had a shameful smell, like wet dog.

"How do you do, Señor Feiler. What a shame about the rain. It has ruined your suit but it gives your face a fine color."

They shook hands, and it came over Clarence with a thrill as he looked at the high-bridged nose and dark, fine-textured skin of del Nido that he was in touch with Gonzaga himself—this round-shouldered man in his linen suit, bowing his sloping head, smiling with sharp teeth, with his hairless hand and big-boned wrist and his awkward fanny, had been Gonzaga's friend and belonged within the legend. Clarence at once sensed that del Nido would make him look foolish if he could, with his irony and his fine Spanish manners. Del Nido was the sort of man who cut everyone down to size. Gonzaga himself would not have been spared by him. *"Go away! You have no holy ones,"* Gonzaga had written.

"The letter I sent you—" Clarence managed to begin. They were hurrying toward the dining room; other guests were waiting.

"We can discuss it later."

"I understand you gave certain poems to the Countess del Camino," he said.

But del Nido was speaking with another guest. The candles were lit and the company sat down.

Clarence had no appetite.

He was sitting between an Italian Monsignore and an Egyptian lady who had lived in New York and spoke very slangy English. There was a German gentleman, too, who headed some insurance company; he sat between Señora del Nido and her daughter. From his end of the table, del Nido with his narrow sleek head and his forward-curved teeth shining with valuable crowns, dominated the conversation. About his eyes the skin was twisted in curious laugh wrinkles. Impressed, appalled, too, Clarence asked himself again and again how Gonzaga could have trusted such a person. A maker of witticisms, as Pascal had said, a bad character. When these words of Pascal came into his head, Clarence turned to the Monsignore as a man to whom this might make sense. But the Monsignore was interested mostly in stamp collecting. Clarence was not, so the Monsignore had nothing further to say to him. He was a gloomy, fleshy man whose hair grew strongly and low over the single deep wrinkle of his forehead.

Guzmán del Nido kept talking. He talked about modern painting, about mystery stories, about old Russia, about the movies, about Nietzsche. Dreamy-looking, the daughter seemed not to listen; the wife expanded some of his remarks. The daughter stared with close-set eyes into the candle flames. The Egyptian lady was amused by the strong smell of Clarence's rain-shrinking clothes. She made a remark about wet wool. He was grateful for the absence of electric lights.

"An American was arrested in Córdoba," said Guzmán del Nido. "He stole the hat of a *Guardia Civil* for a souvenir."

"Isn't that unusual!"

"He'll find the jail smaller than the jails at home. I hope you won't mind if I tell a story about Americans and the size of things in Spain."

"Why should I mind?" said Clarence.

"Splendid. Well, there was an American whose Spanish host could not impress him. Everything was larger in

America. The skyscrapers were bigger than the palaces. The cars were bigger. The cats were bigger. At last his host placed a boiled lobster between his sheets and when the horrified American saw it his host said, 'This is one of our bedbugs.' "

For some reason this fetched Clarence more than it did the others. He uttered a bark of laughter that made the candles flutter.

"Perhaps you'll tell us an American story," said del Nido.

Clarence thought. "Well, here's one," he said. "Two dogs meet in the street. Old friends. One says, 'Hello.' The other answers, 'Cock-a-doodle-do!' 'What does that mean? What's this cock-a-doodle-do stuff?' 'Oh,' says he, 'I've been studying foreign languages.' "

Dead silence. No one laughed. The Egyptian lady said, "I'm afraid you laid an egg." Clarence was angry.

"Is this story told in English or in American?" del Nido asked.

That started a discussion. Was American really a sort of English? Was it a language? No one seemed sure, and Clarence at last, said, "I don't know whether or not it is a language, but there is *something* spoken. I've seen people cry in it and so forth, just as elsewhere."

"We deserved that," said del Nido. "It's true, we're not fair to Americans. In reality the only true Europeans left are Americans."

"How so?"

"The Europeans themselves do not have the peace of mind to appreciate what's best. Life is too hard for us, society too unstable."

Clarence realized that he was being shafted; del Nido was satirizing his guest; he undoubtedly meant that Clarence could not comprehend Gonzaga's poems. An ugly hatred for del Nido grew and knotted in his breast. He wanted to hit him, to strangle him, to trample him, to pick him up and hurl him at the wall. Luckily del Nido was called to the phone, and Clarence stared out his rage at the empty place, the napkin, the silver, the crest of the chair. Only Señorita del Nido seemed aware that he was offended.

Once more Clarence told himself that there was a wrong way to go about obtaining the poems, a way contrary to their spirit. That did much to calm him. He managed to get down a few spoonfuls of ice cream and mastered himself.

"Why are you so interested in Gonzaga?" said del Nido to him later in the garden, under the date palms with their remote leaves.

"I studied Spanish literature in college and became a Gonzagian."

"Wasn't that rather strange, though? You must forgive me, but I see my poor old friend Gonzaga, who was Spanish of the Spanish, in that terrible uniform we used to wear, and our hands and faces bruised and baked and chapped by the desert sun, and I ask myself why he should have had an effect . . ."

"I don't know why. I'd like to understand it myself; but the fact that he did is what you start with."

"I have an interesting observation about poets and their lives. Some are better in real life than in their work. You read bitter poems and then you find the poet is personally very happy and good-tempered. Some are worse in their personality than you would guess from their work. They are luckier, in a way, because they have a chance to correct their faults and improve themselves. Best of all are the ones who are exactly the same inside and out, in the spoken word and the written. To be what you seem to be is the objective of true culture. Gonzaga was of the second type."

"Was he?" It occurred to Clarence that del Nido was trying to make himself more interesting to him than Gonzaga could be and to push Gonzaga out.

"I think I can tell you one reason why Gonzaga appeals to me," said Clarence. "He got away from solving *his* own problem. I often feel this way about it: a poem is great because it is absolutely necessary. Before it came, silence. After it comes, more silence. It begins when it must and ends when it must, and therefore it's not personal. It's 'the sound truly not my own.'" Now he was proving to del Nido that he *could* comprehend; at the same time he knew that he was throwing away his effort. Guzmán del Nido was fundamentally indifferent. Indifferent, indifferent, indifferent! He fundamentally did not care. What can you do with people who don't fundamentally care! "But you know why I came to you. I want to know what became of Gonzaga's last poems. What are they like?"

"They were superb love poems. But I don't know where they are now. They were dedicated to the Countess del Camino and I was supposed to hand them on to her. Which I did."

"There aren't any copies?" said Clarence, trembling as del Nido spoke of the poems.

"No. They were for the Countess."

"Of course. But they were also for everyone else."

"There's plenty of poetry already, for everyone. Homer, Dante, Calderón, Shakespeare. Have you noticed how much difference it makes?"

"It should make a difference. It's not their fault if it doesn't. Besides, Calderón wasn't your friend. But Gonzaga was. Where's the countess now? The poor woman is dead, isn't she? And what happened to those poems? Where do you think they can be?"

"I don't know. She had a secretary named Polvo, a fine old man. A few years ago he died, too. The old man's nephews live in Alcalá de Henares. Where Cervantes was born, you know. They're in the civil service, and they're very decent people, I hear."

"You never even asked them what happened to your friend's poems?" Clarence was astonished. "Didn't you want to find them?"

"I thought eventually I'd try to trace them. I'm sure the countess would have taken good care of her poems."

This was where the discussion stopped, and Clarence was just as glad that it couldn't continue; he sensed that Guzmán del Nido would have liked to give him the dirt on Gonzaga—revelations involving women, drunkenness and dope-taking, bribery, gonorrhea, or even murder. Gonzaga had escaped into the army; that was notorious. But Clarence didn't want to hear del Nido's reminiscences.

It's natural to suppose, because a man is great, that the people around him must have known how to respond to greatness, but when these people turn out to be no better than Guzmán del Nido you wonder what response greatness really needs.

This was what Clarence was saying to Miss Ungar several days later.

"He's glad he doesn't have the poems," said Miss Ungar. "If he had them he'd feel obliged to do something about them, and he's afraid of that because of his official position."

"That's right. Exactly," said Clarence. "But he did me one favor anyway. He put me on to the countess's secretary's nephews. I've written to them and they've invited me to Alcalá de Henares. They didn't mention the poems but maybe they were just being discreet. I'd better start being more discreet myself. There's something unpleasant going on, I think."

"What is it?"

"The police have an eye on me."

"Oh, come!"

"I do. I'm serious. My room was searched yesterday. I

know it was. My landlady didn't answer one way or another when I asked her. She didn't even bother."

"It's too peculiar for anything," Miss Ungar said, laughing in amazement. "But why should they search? What for?"

"I suppose I just inspire suspicion. And then I made a mistake with my landlady the day after my visit to del Nido. She's a very patriotic character. She has a retired general in the *pensión*, too. Well, she was talking to me the other morning and among other things she told me how healthy she was, strong as a rock—*una roca*—a sort of Gibraltar. And, like a dumbbell, I said, without even thinking, '*Gibraltar Español!*' That was an awful boner."

"Why?"

"During the war, you see, when the British were taking such a pounding there was a great agitation for the return of Gibraltar to Spain. The slogan was *Gibraltar Español!* Of course they don't like to be reminded that they were dying for the British to get it good from Germany. Well, she probably thinks I'm a political-secret-somebody. And she was just plain offended."

"But what difference does it really make, as long as you don't do anything terribly illegal?"

"When you're watched closely you're bound sooner or later to do *something*," he said.

He went out to Alcalá on a Sunday afternoon and met the two nephews of Don Francisco Polvo and their wives and daughters.

They proved to be a family of laughers. They laughed when they spoke and when you answered. You saw nothing in the town but sleepy walls, and parched trees and stones. The brothers were squat, sandy-haired, broad-bellied men.

"We're having tea in the garden," said Don Luis Polvo. He was called "the Englishman" by the others because he had lived in London for several months twenty years ago;

they addressed him as "My Lord," and he obliged them by acting like an *Inglés*. He even owned a Scottish terrier named *Duglas*. The family cried to him, "Now's your chance to speak English, Luis. Speak to him!"

"Jolly country, eh?" Luis said. That was about all he could manage.

"Very."

"More, more!"

"Charing Cross," he said.

"Go on, Luis, say more."

"Piccadilly. And that's all I can remember."

The tea was served. Clarence drank and sweltered. Lizards raced in the knotty grapevines and by the well. . . . The wives were embroidering. The laughing daughters were conversing in French, obviously about Clarence. Nobody appeared to believe what he said. Lanky and pained, he sat in what looked to be a suit made of burlap, with his tea. Instead of a saucer, he felt as though he were holding on to the rim of Saturn.

After tea they showed him through the house. It was huge, old, bare, thick-walled and chill, and it was filled with the portraits and the clothing of ancestors—weapons, breastplates, helmets, daggers, guns. In one room where the picture of a general in the Napoleonic Wars was hung, a fun-making mood seized the brothers. They tried on plumed hats, then sabers, and finally full uniforms. Wearing spurs, medals, musty gloves, they went running back to the terrace where the women sat. Don Luis dragged a sword, his seat hung down and the cocked hat sagged broken, opening in the middle on his sandy baldness. With a Napoleonic musket, full of mockery, he performed the manual-of-arms to uproarious laughter. Clarence laughed, too, his cheeks creased; he couldn't explain however why his heart was growing heavier by the minute.

Don Luis aimed the musket and shouted, *"La bomba atómica! Poum!"* The hit he scored with this was enor-

mous. The women shrieked, swiveling their fans, and his
brother fell on his behind in the sanded path, weeping with
laughter. The terrier *Duglas* leaped into Don Luis's face,
fiercely excited.

Don Luis threw a stick and cried, "Fetch, fetch, *Duglas!
La bomba atómica! La bomba atómica!*"

The blood stormed into Clarence's head furiously. This
was another assault on him. Oh! he thought frantically, the
things he had to bear! The punishment he had to take trying to salvage those poems!

As if in the distance, the voice of Don Luis cried, "Hiro-
shima! Nagasaki! Bikini! Good show!" He flung the stick
and the dog bounded on taut legs, little *Duglas*, from the
diminished figure of his master and back—the tiny white-
and-brown animal, while laughter incessantly pierced the
dry air of the garden.

It was not a decent joke, even though Don Luis in that
split hat and the withered coat was mocking the dead military grandeur of his own country. That didn't even the
score. The hideous stun of the bomb and its unbearable,
death-brilliant mushroom cloud filled Clarence's brain.

This was not right. He managed to stop Don Luis. He approached him, laid a hand on the musket, and asked to
speak with him privately. It made the others laugh. The
ladies started to murmur about him. An older woman said,
"*Es gracioso*"; the girls seemed to disagree. He heard one of
them answer, "*Non, il n'est pas gentil.*" Proudly polite, Clarence faced it out. "Damn their damn tea!" he said to himself. His shirt was sticking to his back.

"We did not inherit my uncle's papers," said Don Luis.
"Enough, *Duglas!*" He threw the stick down the well. "My
brother and I inherited this old house and other land, but if
there were papers they probably went to my cousin Pedro
Álvarez-Polvo who lives in Segovia. He's a very interesting
fellow. He works for the *Banco Español* but is a cultivated
person. The countess had no family. She was fond of my

uncle. My uncle was extremely fond of Álvarez-Polvo. They shared the same interests."

"Did your uncle ever speak of Gonzaga?"

"I don't recall. The countess had a large number of artistic admirers. This Gonzaga interests you very much, doesn't he?"

"Yes. Why shouldn't I be interested in him? You may someday be interested in an American poet."

"I? No!" Don Luis laughed, but he was startled.

What people! Damn these dirty laughers! Clarence waited until Don Luis's shocked and latterly somewhat guilty laughter ended, and his broad yap, with spacious teeth, closed—his lips shook with resistance to closing, and finally remained closed.

"Do you think your cousin Álvarez-Polvo would know . . ."

"He would know a lot," said Don Luis, composed. "My uncle confided in him. *He* can tell you something definite, you can count on him. I'll give you a letter of introduction."

"If it's not too much trouble."

"No, no, the pleasure is mine." Don Luis was all courtesy.

After returning to Madrid on the bus through the baking plain of Castile, Clarence phoned Miss Ungar. He wanted her sympathy and comfort. But she didn't invite him to come over. She said, "I can give you the pesetas tomorrow." The pilot had landed, and he thought she sounded regretful. Perhaps she was not really in love with her fiancé. Clarence now had the impression that the black-marketing was not her idea but the pilot's. It embarrassed her. But she was loyal.

"I'll come by later in the week. There's no hurry," he said. "I'm busy anyway."

It would hurt him to do it, but he'd cash a check at the American Express tomorrow at the preposterous legal rate of exchange.

Disappointed, Clarence hung up. *He* should have a woman like that. It passed dimly over his mind that a live woman would make a better quest than a dead poet. But the poet was already *there;* the woman not. He sent a letter to Álvarez-Polvo. He bathed in the sink, and lay reading Gonzaga by a buzzing bulb under the canopy of his bed.

He arrived in Segovia early one Sunday morning. It was filled with sunlight, the clouds were silk-white in the mountain air. Their shadows wandered over the slopes of the bare sierra like creatures that crept and warmed themselves on the soil and rock. All over the old valley were convents, hermitages, churches, towers, the graves of San Juan and other mystical saints. At the highest point of Segovia was the Alcázar of Isabella the Catholic. And passing over the town with its many knobby granite curves that divided the sky was the aqueduct, this noble Roman remnant, as bushy as old men's ears. Clarence stood at the window of his hotel and looked at this conjured rise of stones that bridged the streets. It got him, all of it—the ancient mountain slopes worn as if by the struggles of Jacob with the angel, the spires, the dry glistening of the atmosphere, the hermit places in green hideaways, the sheep-bells' clunk, the cistern water dropping, while beams came as straight as harp wires from the sun. All of this, like a mild weight, seemed to press on him; it opened him up. He felt his breath creep within him like a tiny pet animal.

He went down through the courtyard. There the cistern of fat stone held green water, full of bottom-radiations from the golden brass of the faucets. Framed above it in an archway were ladies' hair styles of twenty years ago—a brilliantine advertisement. Ten or so beautiful *señoritas* with bangs, shingles, and windswept bobs, smiling like priestesses of love. Therefore Clarence had the idea that this cistern was the Fountain of Youth. And also that it was something Arcadian. He said, " 'Ye glorious nymphs!' " and burst out laughing. He felt happy—magnificent! The sun poured over his head and embraced his back hotly.

Smiling, he rambled up and down the streets. He went to the Alcázar. Soldiers in German helmets were on guard. He went to the cathedral. It was ancient but the stones looked brand-new. After lunch he sat at the café in front of the aqueduct waiting for Álvarez-Polvo. On the wide sloping sidewalk there were hundreds of folding chairs, empty, the paint blazed off them and the wood emerging as gray as silverfish. The long low windows were open, so that inside and outside mingled, the yellow and the somber, the bar brown and the sky clear blue. A gypsy woman came out and gave Clarence the eye. She was an entertainer, but whether a real gypsy or not was conjectural. In the phrase he had heard, some of these girls were *gitanas de miedo*, fear-inspiring, or strictly from hunger. But he sat and studied the aqueduct, trying to imagine what sort of machinery they could have used to raise the stones.

A black hearse with mourners who trod after it slowly, and with all the plumes, and carvings of angels and death-grimacers, went through the main arch to the cemetery. After ten minutes it came galloping back with furious lashing of the horses, the silk-hatted coachman standing, yacking at them. Only a little later the same hearse returned with another procession of mourners who supported one another, weeping aloud, grief pushing on their backs. Through the arch again. And once more the hearse came flying back. With a sudden tightness of the guts Clarence thought, Why all these burials at once? Was there a plague? He looked at the frothy edge of his glass. Not very clean!

But Álvarez-Polvo set his mind at rest. He said, "The hearse was broken all week. It has just been repaired. A week's dead to bury."

He was a strange-looking man. His face seemed to have been worked by three or four diseases and then abandoned.

His nose swelled out, shrinking his eyes. He had a huge mouth, like Cousin Don Luis. He wore a beret, and a yellow silk sash was wound about his belly. Clarence often had noticed that short men with big bellies sometimes held their arms ready for defense as they walked, but at heart apparently expected defeat. Álvarez-Polvo, too, had that posture. His face, brown, mottled, creased, sunlit, was edged with kinky gray hair escaping from the beret. His belly was like a drum, and he seemed also to have a drumlike soul. If you struck, you wouldn't injure him. You'd hear a sound.

"You know what I've come for?" said Clarence.

"Yes, I do know. But let's not start talking business right away. You've never been in Segovia before, I assume, and you must let me be hospitable. I'm a proud Segoviano—proud of this ancient, beautiful city, and it would give me pleasure to show you the principal places."

At the words "talking business" Clarence's heart rose a notch. Was it only a matter of settling the price? Then he had the poems! Something in Clarence flapped with eager joy, like a flag in the wind.

"By all means. For a while. It is beautiful. Never in my life have I seen anything so gorgeous as Segovia."

Álvarez-Polvo took his arm.

"With me you will not only see, you will also understand. I have made a study of it. I'm a lover of such things. I seldom have an opportunity to express it. Wherever I take my wife, she is interested only in *novelas morbosas*. At Versailles she sat and read Ellery Queen. In Paris, the same. In Rome, the same. If she lives to the end of time, she will never run out of *novelas morbosas*."

From this remark, without notice, he took a deep plunge into the subject of women, and he carried Clarence with him. Women, women, women! All the types of Spanish beauty. The Granadinas, the Malagueñas, the Castellanas, the Cataluñas. And then the Germans, the Greeks, the French, the Swedes! He tightened his hold on Clarence and

pulled him close as he boasted and complained and cata-
logued and confessed. He was ruined! They had taken his
money, his health, his time, his years, his life, women had
—innocent, mindless, beautiful, ravaging, insidious, ma-
levolent, chestnut, blond, red, black. . . . Clarence felt
hemmed in by women's faces, and by women's bodies.

"I suppose you'd call this a Romanesque church,
wouldn't you?" Clarence said, stopping.

"Of course it is," said Álvarez-Polvo. "Just notice how the
Renaissance building next to it was designed to harmonize
with it."

Clarence was looking at the pillars and their blunted
faces of humorous, devil-beast humanities, the stone birds,
demon lollers and apostles. Two men carried by a bedspring
and a mattress in a pushcart. They looked like the kings of
Shinar and Elam defeated by Abraham.

"Come, have a glass of wine," said Álvarez-Polvo. "I'm
not allowed to drink since my operation, but you must have
something."

When would they begin to talk about the poems? Clarence was impatient. Gonzaga's poems would mean little if
anything to a man like this, but in spite of his endless gal-
lant bunk and his swagger and his complaints about having broken his springs in the service of love and beauty, he
was probably a very cunning old fuff. He wanted to stall
Clarence and find out what the poems were worth to him.
And so Clarence gazed, or blinked, straight ahead, and kept
a tight grip on his feelings.

In the *bodega* were huge barrels, copper fittings, innu-
merable bottles duplicated in the purple mirror, platters of
mariscos, crawfish bugging their eyes on stalks, their feel-
ers cooked into various last shapes. From the middle of the
floor rose a narrow spiral staircase. It mounted—who-knew-
where? Clarence tried to see but couldn't. A little torn-
frocked beggar child came selling lottery tickets. The old

chaser petted her; she wheedled; she took his small hand and laid her cheek to it. Still talking, he felt her hair. He stroked his fill and sent her away with a coin.

Clarence drank down the sweet, yellow Malaga.

"Now," said Álvarez-Polvo, "I will show you a church few visitors ever see."

They descended to the lower part of town, down littered stairways of stone, by cavelike homes and a vacant lot where runty boys were butting a football with their heads, and dribbling and hooking it with their boots.

"Here," Álvarez-Polvo said. "This wall is of the tenth century and this one of the seventeenth."

The air inside the church was dark, cool, thick as ointment. Hollows of dark red and dark blue and heavy yellow slowly took shape, and Clarence began to see the altar, the columns.

Álvarez-Polvo was silent. The two men were standing before a harshly crowned Christ. The figure was gored deeply in the side, rust-blooded. The crown of thorns was too wide and heavy to be borne. As he confronted it, Clarence felt that it threatened to scratch the life out of him, to scratch him to the heart.

"The matter that interests us both . . ." Álvarez-Polvo then said.

"Yes, yes, let's go somewhere and have a talk about it. You found the poems among your uncle's papers. Do you have them here in Segovia?"

"Poems?" said Álvarez-Polvo, turning the dark and ruined face from the aisle. "That's a strange word to use for them."

"Do you mean they're not in that form? What are they then? What are they written in?"

"Why, the usual legal language. According to law."

"I don't understand."

"Neither do I. But I can show you what I'm talking about.

Here. I have one with me. I brought it along." He drew a document from his pocket.

Clarence held it, trembling. It was heavy—glossy and heavy. He felt an embossed surface. Yes, there was a seal on it. What had the countess done with the poems? Had them engraved? This paper was emblazoned with a gilt star. He sought light and read, within an elaborate border of wavy green, *Compañia de Minas, S.A.*

"Is this— It can't be. You've given me the wrong thing." His heart was racing. "Put it back. Look in your pocket again."

"Why the wrong thing?"

"It looks like shares of stock."

"It's what it's supposed to be, mining stock. Isn't that what you're interested in?"

"Of course not! Certainly not! What kind of mine?"

"It's a pitchblende mine in Morocco, that's what it is."

"What do I want with pitchblende?" Clarence said.

"What any businessman would want. To sell it. Pitchblende has uranium in it. Uranium is used in atom bombs."

Oh, dear God!

"Claro. Para la bomba atómica."

"What have I to do with atom bombs? What do I care about atom bombs! To hell with atom bombs!" said Clarence.

"I understood you were a financier."

"Me? Do I look like one?"

"Yes, of course you do. More an English than an American financier I thought. But a financier. Aren't you?"

"I am not. I came about the poems of Gonzaga, the poems owned by the Countess del Camino. Love poems dedicated to her by the poet Manuel Gonzaga."

"Manuel? The soldier? The little fellow? The one that was her lover in nineteen twenty-eight? He was killed in Morocco."

"Yes, yes! What did your uncle do with the poems?"

"Oh, that's what you were talking about. Why, my uncle did nothing with them. The countess did, herself. She had the poems buried with her. She took them to the grave."

"Buried! With her, you say! And no copies?"

"I doubt it. My uncle had instructions from her, and he was very loyal. He lived by loyalty. My uncle—"

"Oh, damn! Oh, damn it! And didn't he leave you anything in that collection of papers that has to do with Gonzaga? No journals, no letters that mention Gonzaga? Nothing?"

"He left me these shares in the mine. They're valuable. Not yet, but they will be if I can get capital. But you can't raise money in Spain. Spanish capital is cowardly, ignorant of science. It is still in the Counter Reformation. Let me show you the location of this mine." He opened a map and began to explain the geography of the Atlas Mountains.

Clarence walked out on him—ran, rather. Panting, enraged, he climbed from the lower town.

As soon as he entered his room at the hotel he knew that his valise had been searched. Storming, he slammed it shut and dragged it down the stairs, past the cistern, and into the lobby.

He shouted to the manager, "Why must the police come and turn my things upside down?"

White-faced and stern, the manager said, "You must be mistaken, *señor*."

"I am not mistaken. They searched my wastebasket."

A man rose angrily from a chair in the lobby. In an old suit, he wore a mourning band on his arm.

"These Englishmen!" he said with fury. "They don't know what hospitality is. They come here and enjoy themselves, and criticize our country, and complain about Spanish police. What hypocrisy! There are more police in England than in Spain. The whole world knows you have a huge jail in Liverpool, filled with Masons. Five thousand Masons are *encarcelados* in Liverpool alone."

There was nothing to say. All the way to Madrid Clarence sat numb and motionless in his second-class seat.

As the train left the mountains, the heavens seemed to split. Rain began to fall, heavy and sudden, boiling on the wide plain.

He knew what to expect from that redheaded Miss Walsh at dinner.

A FATHER-TO-BE

The strangest notions had a way of forcing themselves into Rogin's mind. Just thirty-one and passable-looking, with short black hair, small eyes, but a high, open forehead, he was a research chemist, and his mind was generally serious and dependable. But on a snowy Sunday evening while this stocky man, buttoned to the chin in a Burberry coat and walking in his preposterous gait—feet turned outward—was going toward the subway, he fell into a peculiar state.

He was on his way to have supper with his fiancée. She had phoned him a short while ago and said, "You'd better pick up a few things on the way."

"What do we need?"

"Some roast beef, for one thing. I bought a quarter of a pound coming home from my aunt's."

"Why a quarter of a pound, Joan?" said Rogin, deeply

annoyed. "That's just about enough for one good sandwich."

"So you have to stop at a delicatessen. I had no more money."

He was about to ask, "What happened to the thirty dollars I gave you on Wednesday?" but he knew that would not be right.

"I had to give Phyllis money for the cleaning woman," said Joan.

Phyllis, Joan's cousin, was a young divorcee, extremely wealthy. The two women shared an apartment.

"Roast beef," he said, "and what else?"

"Some shampoo, sweetheart. We've used up all the shampoo. And hurry, darling, I've missed you all day."

"And I've missed you," said Rogin, but to tell the truth he had been worrying most of the time. He had a younger brother whom he was putting through college. And his mother, whose annuity wasn't quite enough in these days of inflation and high taxes, needed money too. Joan had debts he was helping her to pay, for she wasn't working. She was looking for something suitable to do. Beautiful, well educated, aristocratic in her attitude, she couldn't clerk in a dime store; she couldn't model clothes (Rogin thought this made girls vain and stiff, and he didn't want her to); she couldn't be a waitress or a cashier. What could she be? Well, something would turn up and meantime Rogin hesitated to complain. He paid her bills—the dentist, the department store, the osteopath, the doctor, the psychiatrist. At Christmas, Rogin almost went mad. Joan bought him a velvet smoking jacket with frog fasteners, a beautiful pipe, and a pouch. She bought Phyllis a garnet brooch, an Italian silk umbrella, and a gold cigarette holder. For other friends, she bought Dutch pewter and Swedish glassware. Before she was through, she had spent five hundred dollars of Rogin's money. He loved her too much to show his suffering. He believed she had a far better nature than his. She didn't worry about money. She had a marvelous character, always cheerful, and she really didn't need a psychiatrist at all. She went to one because Phyllis did and it made her curious. She tried too much to keep up with her cousin, whose father had made millions in the rug business.

While the woman in the drugstore was wrapping the shampoo bottle, a clear idea suddenly arose in Rogin's thoughts: Money surrounds you in life as the earth does in death. Superimposition is the universal law. Who is free? No one is free. Who has no burdens? Everyone is under pressure. The very rocks, the waters of the earth, beasts, men, children—everyone has some weight to carry. This idea was extremely clear to him at first. Soon it became rather vague, but it had a great effect nevertheless, as if someone had given him a valuable gift. (Not like the velvet smoking jacket he couldn't bring himself to wear, or the pipe it choked him to smoke.) The notion that all were under pressure and affliction, instead of saddening him, had the opposite influence. It put him in a wonderful mood. It was extraordinary how happy he became and, in addition, clear-sighted. His eyes all at once were opened to what was around him. He saw with delight how the druggist and the woman who wrapped the shampoo bottle were smiling and flirting, how the lines of worry in her face went over into lines of cheer and the druggist's receding gums did not hinder his kidding and friendliness. And in the delicatessen, also, it was amazing how much Rogin noted and what happiness it gave him simply to be there.

Delicatessens on Sunday night, when all other stores are shut, will overcharge you ferociously, and Rogin would normally have been on guard, but he was not tonight, or scarcely so. Smells of pickle, sausage, mustard, and smoked fish overjoyed him. He pitied the people who would buy the chicken salad and chopped herring; they could do it only because their sight was too dim to see what they were getting—the fat flakes of pepper on the chicken, the soppy herring, mostly vinegar-soaked stale bread. Who would buy them? Late risers, people living alone, waking up in the darkness of the afternoon, finding their refrigerators empty, or people whose gaze was turned inward. The roast beef looked not bad, and Rogin ordered a pound.

While the storekeeper was slicing the meat, he yelled at a Puerto Rican kid who was reaching for a bag of chocolate cookies, "Hey, you want to pull me down the whole display on yourself? You, *chico*, wait a half a minute." This storekeeper, though he looked like one of Pancho Villa's bandits, the kind that smeared their enemies with syrup and staked them down on anthills, a man with toadlike eyes and stout hands made to clasp pistols hung around his belly, was not so bad. He was a New York man, thought Rogin—who was from Albany himself—a New York man toughened by every abuse of the city, trained to suspect everyone. But in his own realm, on the board behind the counter, there was justice. Even clemency.

The Puerto Rican kid wore a complete cowboy outfit—a green hat with white braid, guns, chaps, spurs, boots, and gauntlets—but he couldn't speak any English. Rogin unhooked the cellophane bag of hard circular cookies and gave it to him. The boy tore the cellophane with his teeth and began to chew one of those dry chocolate disks. Rogin recognized his state—the energetic dream of childhood. Once, he, too, had found these dry biscuits delicious. It would have bored him now to eat one.

What else would Joan like? Rogin thought fondly. Some strawberries? "Give me some frozen strawberries. No, raspberries, she likes those better. And heavy cream. And some rolls, cream cheese, and some of those rubber-looking gherkins."

"What rubber?"

"Those, deep green, with eyes. Some ice cream might be in order, too."

He tried to think of a compliment, a good comparison,

an endearment, for Joan when she'd open the door. What about her complexion? There was really nothing to compare her sweet, small, daring, shapely, timid, defiant, loving face to. How difficult she was, and how beautiful!

As Rogin went down into the stony, odorous, metallic, captive air of the subway, he was diverted by an unusual confession made by a man to his friend. These were two very tall men, shapeless in their winter clothes, as if their coats concealed suits of chain mail.

"So, how long have you known me?" said one.

"Twelve years."

"Well, I have an admission to make," he said. "I've decided that I might as well. For years I've been a heavy drinker. You didn't know. Practically an alcoholic."

But his friend was not surprised, and he answered immediately, "Yes, I did know."

"You knew? Impossible! How could you?"

Why, thought Rogin, as if it could be a secret! Look at that long, austere, alcohol-washed face, that drink-ruined nose, the skin by his ears like turkey wattles, and those whisky-saddened eyes.

"Well, I did know, though."

"You couldn't have. I can't believe it." He was upset, and his friend didn't seem to want to soothe him. "But it's all right now," he said. "I've been going to a doctor and taking pills, a new revolutionary Danish discovery. It's a miracle. I'm beginning to believe they can cure you of anything and everything. You can't beat the Danes in science. They do everything. They turned a man into a woman."

"That isn't how they stop you from drinking, is it?"

"No. I hope not. This is only like aspirin. It's superaspirin. They called it the aspirin of the future. But if you use it, you have to stop drinking."

Rogin's illuminated mind asked of itself while the human tides of the subway swayed back and forth, and cars linked and transparent like fish bladders raced under the streets:

How come he thought nobody would know what everybody couldn't help knowing? And, as a chemist, he asked himself what kind of compound this new Danish drug might be, and started thinking about various inventions of his own, synthetic albumen, a cigarette that lit itself, a cheaper motor fuel. Ye gods, but he needed money! As never before. What was to be done? His mother was growing more and more difficult. On Friday night, she had neglected to cut up his meat for him, and he was hurt. She had sat at the table motionless, with her long-suffering face, severe, and let him cut his own meat, a thing she almost never did. She had always spoiled him and made his brother envy him. But what she expected now! Oh, Lord, how he had to pay, and it had never even occurred to him formerly that these things might have a price.

Seated, one of the passengers, Rogin recovered his calm, happy, even clairvoyant state of mind. To think of money was to think as the world wanted you to think; then you'd never be your own master. When people said they wouldn't do something for love or money, they meant that love and money were opposite passions and one the enemy of the other. He went on to reflect how little people knew about this, how they slept through life, how small a light the light of consciousness was. Rogin's clean, snub-nosed face shone while his heart was torn with joy at these deeper thoughts of our ignorance. You might take this drunkard as an example, who for long years thought his closest friends never suspected he drank. Rogin looked up and down the aisle for this remarkable knightly symbol, but he was gone.

However, there was no lack of things to see. There was a small girl with a new white muff; into the muff a doll's head was sewn, and the child was happy and affectionately vain of it, while her old man, stout and grim, with a huge scowling nose, kept picking her up and resettling her in the seat, as if he were trying to change her into something else. Then another child, led by her mother, boarded the car, and this other child carried the very same doll-faced muff, and this greatly annoyed both parents. The woman, who looked like a difficult, contentious woman, took her daughter away. It seemed to Rogin that each child was in love with its own muff and didn't even see the other, but it was one of his foibles to think he understood the hearts of little children.

A foreign family next engaged his attention. They looked like Central Americans to him. On one side the mother, quite old, dark-faced, white-haired, and worn out; on the other a son with the whitened, porous hands of a dish-washer. But what was the dwarf who sat between them—a son or a daughter? The hair was long and wavy and the cheeks smooth, but the shirt and tie were masculine. The overcoat was feminine, but the shoes—the shoes were a puzzle. A pair of brown oxfords with an outer seam like a man's, but Baby Louis heels like a woman's—a plain toe like a man's, but a strap across the instep like a woman's. No stockings. That didn't help much. The dwarf's fingers were beringed, but without a wedding band. There were small grim dents in the cheeks. The eyes were puffy and concealed, but Rogin did not doubt that they could reveal strange things if they chose and that this was a creature of remarkable understanding. He had for many years owned de la Mare's *Memoirs of a Midget*. Now he took a resolve; he would read it. As soon as he had decided, he was free from his consuming curiosity as to the dwarf's sex and was able to look at the person who sat beside him.

Thoughts very often grow fertile in the subway, because of the motion, the great company, the subtlety of the rider's state as he rattles under streets and rivers, under the foundations of great buildings, and Rogin's mind had already been strangely stimulated. Clasping the bag of groceries from which there rose odors of bread and pickle spice, he was following a train of reflections, first about the chemistry of sex determination, the X and Y chromosomes, hereditary linkages, the uterus, afterward about his brother as a tax exemption. He recalled two dreams of the night before. In one, an undertaker had offered to cut his hair, and he had refused. In another, he had been carrying a woman on his head. Sad dreams, both! Very sad! Which was the woman—Joan or Mother? And the undertaker—his lawyer? He gave a deep sigh, and by force of habit began to put together his synthetic albumen that was to revolutionize the entire egg industry.

Meanwhile, he had not interrupted his examination of the passengers and had fallen into a study of the man next to him. This was a man whom he had never in his life seen before but with whom he now suddenly felt linked through all existence. He was middle-aged, sturdy, with clear skin and blue eyes. His hands were clean, well formed, but Rogin did not approve of them. The coat he wore was a fairly expensive blue check such as Rogin would never have chosen for himself. He would not have worn blue suède shoes, either, or such a faultless hat, a cumbersome felt animal of a hat encircled by a high, fat ribbon. There are all kinds of dandies, not all of them are of the flaunting kind; some are dandies of respectability, and Rogin's fellow passenger was one of these. His straight-nosed profile was handsome, yet he had betrayed his gift, for he was flat-looking. But in his flat way he seemed to warn people that he wanted no difficulties with them, he wanted nothing to do with them. Wearing such blue suède shoes, he could not afford to have people treading on his feet, and he seemed to draw about himself a circle of privilege, notifying all others to mind their own business and let him read his paper. He was holding a *Tribune*, and perhaps it would be overstatement to say that he was reading. He was holding it.

His clear skin and blue eyes, his straight and purely Roman nose—even the way he sat—all strongly suggested one person to Rogin: Joan. He tried to escape the comparison, but it couldn't be helped. This man not only looked like Joan's father, whom Rogin detested; he looked like Joan herself. Forty years hence, a son of hers, provided she had one, might be like this. A son of hers? Of such a son, he himself, Rogin, would be the father. Lacking in dominant traits as compared with Joan, his heritage would not appear. Probably the children would resemble her. Yes, think forty years ahead, and a man like this, who sat by him knee to knee in the hurtling car among their fellow creatures, unconscious participants in a sort of great carnival of transit—such a man would carry forward what had been Rogin.

This was why he felt bound to him through all existence. What were forty years reckoned against eternity! Forty years were gone, and he was gazing at his own son. Here he was. Rogin was frightened and moved. "My son! My son!" he said to himself, and the pity of it almost made him burst into tears. The holy and frightful work of the masters of life and death brought this about. We were their instruments. We worked toward ends we thought were our own. But no! The whole thing was so unjust. To suffer, to labor, to toil and force your way through the spikes of life, to crawl through its darkest caverns, to push through the worst, to struggle under the weight of economy, to make money—only to become the father of a fourth-rate man of the world like this, so flat-looking with his ordinary, clean, rosy, uninteresting, self-satisfied, fundamentally bourgeois face. What a curse to have a dull son! A son like this, who could never understand his father. They had absolutely nothing, but nothing, in common, he and this neat, chubby, blue-eyed man. He was so pleased, thought Rogin, with all he owned and all he did and all he was that he could hardly unfasten his lip. Look at that lip, sticking up at the tip like a little thorn or egg tooth. He wouldn't give anyone the time of day. Would this perhaps be general forty years from now? Would personalities be chillier as the world aged and grew colder? The inhumanity of the next generation incensed Rogin. Father and son had no sign to make to each other. Terrible! Inhuman! What a vision of existence it gave him. Man's personal aims were nothing, illusion. The life force occupied each of us in turn in its progress toward its own fulfillment, trampling on our individual humanity, using us for its own ends like mere dinosaurs or bees, exploiting love heartlessly, making us engage in the social process, labor, struggle for money, and submit to the law of pressure, the universal law of layers, superimposition!

What the blazes am I getting into? Rogin thought. To be the father of a throwback to *her* father. The image of this white-haired, gross, peevish, old man with his ugly selfish blue eyes revolted Rogin. This was how his grandson would look. Joan, with whom Rogin was now more and more displeased, could not help that. For her, it was inevitable. But did it have to be inevitable for him? Well, then, Rogin, you fool, don't be a damned instrument. Get out of the way!

But it was too late for this, because he had already experienced the sensation of sitting next to his own son, his son and Joan's. He kept staring at him, waiting for him to say something, but the presumptive son remained coldly silent though he must have been aware of Rogin's scrutiny. They even got out at the same stop—Sheridan Square. When they stepped to the platform, the man, without even looking at Rogin, went away in a different direction in his detestable blue-checked coat, with his rosy, nasty face.

The whole thing upset Rogin very badly. When he approached Joan's door and heard Phyllis's little dog Henri barking even before he could knock, his face was very tense. I won't be used, he declared to himself. I have my own right to exist. Joan had better watch out. She had a light way of by-passing grave questions he had given earnest thought to. She always assumed no really disturbing thing would happen. He could not afford the luxury of such a carefree, debonair attitude himself, because he had to work hard and earn money so that disturbing things would *not* happen. Well, at the moment this situation could not be helped, and he really did not mind the money if he could feel that she was not necessarily the mother of such a son as his subway son or entirely the daughter of that awful, obscene father of hers. After all, Rogin was not himself so much like either of his parents, and quite different from his brother.

Joan came to the door, wearing one of Phyllis's expensive housecoats. It suited her very well. At first sight of her happy face, Rogin was brushed by the shadow of resemblance; the touch of it was extremely light, almost figmentary, but it made his flesh tremble.

She began to kiss him, saying, "Oh, my baby. You're covered with snow. Why didn't you wear your hat? It's all over its little head"—her favorite third-person endearment.

"Well, let me put down this bag of stuff. Let me take off my coat," grumbled Rogin, and escaped from her embrace. Why couldn't she wait making up to him? "It's so hot in here. My face is burning. Why do you keep the place at this temperature? And that damned dog keeps barking. If you didn't keep it cooped up, it wouldn't be so spoiled and noisy. Why doesn't anybody ever walk him?"

"Oh, it's not really so hot here! You've just come in from the cold. Don't you think this housecoat fits me better than Phyllis? Especially across the hips. She thinks so, too. She may sell it to me."

"I hope not," Rogin almost exclaimed.

She brought a towel to dry the melting snow from his short black hair. The flurry of rubbing excited Henri intolerably, and Joan locked him up in the bedroom, where he jumped persistently against the door with a rhythmic sound of claws on the wood.

Joan said, "Did you bring the shampoo?"

"Here it is."

"Then I'll wash your hair before dinner. Come."

"I don't want it washed."

"Oh, come on," she said, laughing.

Her lack of consciousness of guilt amazed him. He did not see how it could be. And the carpeted, furnished, lamp-lit, curtained room seemed to stand against his vision. So that he felt accusing and angry, his spirit sore and bitter, but it did not seem fitting to say why. Indeed, he began to worry lest the reason for it all slip away from him.

They took off his coat and his shirt in the bathroom, and she filled the sink. Rogin was full of his troubled emotions; now that his chest was bare he could feel them even more and he said to himself, I'll have a thing or two to tell her pretty soon. I'm not letting them get away with it. "Do you think," he was going to tell her, "that I alone was made to carry the burden of the whole world on me? Do you think I was born to be taken advantage of and sacrificed? Do you think I'm just a natural resource, like a coal mine, or oil well, or fishery, or the like? Remember, that I'm a man is no reason why I should be loaded down. I have a soul in me no bigger or stronger than yours.

"Take away the externals, like the muscles, deeper voice, and so forth, and what remains? A pair of spirits, practically alike. So why shouldn't there also be equality? I can't always be the strong one."

"Sit here," said Joan, bringing up a kitchen stool to the sink. "Your hair's gotten all matted."

He sat with his breast against the cool enamel, his chin on the edge of the basin, the green, hot, radiant water reflecting the glass and the tile, and the sweet, cool, fragrant juice of the shampoo poured on his head. She began to wash him.

"You have the healthiest-looking scalp," she said. "It's all pink."

He answered, "Well, it should be white. There must be something wrong with me."

"But there's absolutely nothing wrong with you," she

said, and pressed against him from behind, surrounding him, pouring the water gently over him until it seemed to him that the water came from within him, it was the warm fluid of his own secret loving spirit overflowing into the sink, green and foaming, and the words he had rehearsed he forgot, and his anger at his son-to-be disappeared altogether, and he sighed, and said to her from the water-filled hollow of the sink, "You always have such wonderful ideas, Joan. You know? You have a kind of instinct, a regular gift."

MOSBY'S MEMOIRS

The birds chirped away. Fweet, Fweet, Bootchee-Fweet.
Doing all the things naturalists say they do. Expressing
abysmal depths of aggression, which only Man—Stupid
Man—heard as innocence. We feel everything is so innocent—because our wickedness is so fearful. Oh, very fearful!

Mr. Willis Mosby, after his siesta, gazing down-
mountain at the town of Oaxaca where all were snoozing
still—mouths, rumps, long black Indian hair, the antique
beauty photographically celebrated by Eisenstein in *Thun-
der over Mexico*. Mr. Mosby—Dr. Mosby really; erudite,
maybe even profound; thought much, accomplished much
—had made some of the most interesting mistakes a man
could make in the twentieth century. He was in Oaxaca
now to write his memoirs. He had a grant for the purpose,
from the Guggenheim Foundation. And why not?

Bougainvillaea poured down the hillside, and the hum-
mingbirds were spinning. Mosby felt ill with all this whirl-

ing, these colors, fragrances, ready to topple on him. Liveliness, beauty, seemed very dangerous. Mortal danger. Maybe he had drunk too much mescal at lunch (beer, also). Behind the green and red of Nature, dull black seemed to be thickly laid like mirror backing.

Mosby did not feel quite well; his teeth, gripped tight, made the muscles stand out in his handsome, elderly tanned jaws. He had fine blue eyes, light-pained, direct, intelligent, disbelieving; hair still thick, parted in the middle; and strong vertical grooves between the brows, beneath the nostrils, and at the back of the neck.

The time had come to put some humor into the memoirs. So far it had been: Fundamentalist family in Missouri— Father the successful builder—Early schooling—The State University—Rhodes Scholarship—Intellectual friendships —What I learned from Professor Collingwood—Empire and the mental vigor of Britain—My unorthodox interpretation of John Locke—I work for William Randolph Hearst in Spain—The personality of General Franco—Radical friendships in New York—Wartime service with the O.S.S. —The limited vision of Franklin D. Roosevelt—Comte, Proudhon, and Marx revisited— de Tocqueville once again.

Nothing very funny here. And yet thousands of students and others would tell you, "Mosby had a great sense of humor." Would tell their children, "This Mosby in the O.S.S.," or "Willis Mosby, who was in Toledo with me when the Alcázar fell, made me die laughing." "I shall never forget Mosby's observations on Harold Laski." "On packing the Supreme Court." "On the Russian purge trials." "On Hitler."

So it was certainly high time to do something. He had given it some consideration. He would say, when they sent down his ice from the hotel bar (he was in a cottage below the main building, flowers heaped upon it; envying a little the unencumbered mountains of the Sierra Madre) and when he had chilled his mescal—warm, it tasted rotten— he would write that in 1947, when he was living in Paris, he knew any number of singular people. He knew the Comte de la Mine-Crevée, who sheltered Gary Davis the World Citizen after the World Citizen had burnt his passport publicly. He knew Mr. Julian Huxley at UNESCO. He discussed social theory with Mr. Lévi-Straus but was not invited to dinner—they ate at the Musée de l'Homme. Sartre refused to meet with him; he thought all Americans, Negroes excepted, were secret agents. Mosby for his part suspected all Russians abroad of working for the G.P.U. Mosby knew French well; extremely fluent in Spanish; quite good in German. But the French cannot identify originality in foreigners. That is the curse of an old civilization. It is a heavier planet. Its best minds must double their horsepower to overcome the gravitational field of tradition. Only a few will ever fly. To fly away from Descartes. To fly away from the political anachronisms of left, center, and right persisting since 1789. Mosby found these French exceedingly banal. These French found him lean and tight. In well-tailored clothes, elegant and dry, his good Western skin, pale eyes, strong nose, handsome mouth, and virile creases. *Un type sec.*

Both sides—Mosby and the French, that is—with highly developed attitudes. Both, he was lately beginning to concede, quite wrong. Possibly equidistant from the truth, but lying in different sectors of error. The French were worse off because their errors were collective. Mine, Mosby believed, were at least peculiar. The French were furious over the collapse in 1940 of *La France Pourrie*, their lack of military will, the extensive collaboration, the massive deportations unopposed (the Danes, even the *Bulgarians* resisted Jewish deportations), and, finally, over the humiliation of liberation by the Allies. Mosby, in the O.S.S., had information to support such views. Within the State Department, too, he had university colleagues—former students and old acquaintances. He had expected a high postwar appointment, for which, as director of counter-espio-

nage in Latin America, he was ideally qualified. But Dean
Acheson personally disliked him. Nor did Dulles approve.
Mosby, a fanatic about *ideas*, displeased the institutional
gentry. He had said that the Foreign Service was staffed by
rejects of the power structure. Young gentlemen from
good Eastern colleges who couldn't make it as Wall Street
lawyers were allowed to interpret the alleged interests of
their class in the State Department bureaucracy. In foreign
consulates they could be rude to D.P.s and indulge their
country-club anti-Semitism, which was dying out even in
the country clubs. Besides, Mosby had sympathized with
the Burnham position on managerialism, declaring, during
the war, that the Nazis were winning because they had
made their managerial revolution first. No Allied combina-
tion could conquer, with its obsolete industrialism, a nation which had reached a new state of history and tapped
the power of the inevitable, etc. And then Mosby, holding
forth in Washington, among the elite Scotch drinkers,
stated absolutely that however deplorable the concentration
camps had been, they showed at least the rationality of
German political ideas. The Americans had no such ideas.
They didn't know what they were doing. No design existed.
The British were not much better. The Hamburg fire-bomb-
ing, he argued in his clipped style, in full declarative
phrases, betrayed the idiotic emptiness and planlessness of
Western leadership. Finally, he said that when Acheson
blew his nose there were maggots in his handkerchie.'.

Among the defeated French, Mosby admitted that he had
a galled spirit. (His jokes were not too bad.) And of course
he drank a lot. He worked on Marx and Tocqueville, and
he drank. He would not cease from mental strife. The
Comte de la Mine-Crevée (Mosby's own improvisation on a
noble and ancient name) kept him in PX booze and exchanged his money on the black market for him. He de-
scribed his swindles and was very entertaining.

Mosby now wished to say, in the vein of Sir Harold Nic-

olson or Santayana or Bertrand Russell, writers for whose
memoirs he had the greatest admiration, that Paris in
1947, like half a Noah's Ark, was waiting for the second of
each kind to arrive. There was one of everything. Something of this sort. Especially among Americans. The city
was very bitter, grim; the Seine looked and smelled like
medicine. At an American party, a former student of
French from Minnesota, now running a shady enterprise,
an agency which specialized in bribery, private undercover
investigations, and procuring broads for V.I.P.s, said something highly emotional about the City of Man, about the
meaning of Europe for Americans, the American failure to
preserve human scale. Not omitting to work in Man the
Measure. And every other tag he could bring back from
Randall's *Making of the Modern Mind* or *Readings in the
Intellectual History of Europe*. "I was tempted," Mosby
meant to say (the ice arrived in a glass jar with tongs; the
natives no longer wore the dirty white drawers of the past).
"Tempted . . ." He rubbed his forehead, which projected
like the back of an observation car. "To tell this sententious
little drunkard and gyp artist, formerly a pacifist and vege-
tarian, follower of Gandhi at the University of Minnesota,
now driving a very handsome Bentley to the Tour d'Argent
to eat duck *à l'orange*. Tempted to say, 'Yes, but we come
here across the Atlantic to relax a bit in the past. To recall
what Ezra Pound had once said. That we would make another Venice, just for the hell of it, in the Jersey marshes
any time we liked. Toying. To divert ourselves in the time
of colossal mastery to come. Reproducing anything, for fun.
Baboons trained to row will bring us in gondolas to discussions of astrophysics. Where folks burn garbage now, and
fatten pigs and junk their old machines, we will debark to
hear a concert.' "

Mosby the thinker, like other busy men, never had time
for music. Poetry was not his cup of tea. Members of Con-
gress, Cabinet officers, Organization Men, Pentagon plan-

ners, Party leaders, Presidents had no such interests. They could not be what they were and read Eliot, hear Vivaldi, Cimarosa. But they planned that others might enjoy these things and benefit by their power. Mosby perhaps had more in common with political leaders and Joint Chiefs and Presidents. At least, they were in his thoughts more often than Cimarosa and Eliot. With hate, he pondered their mistakes, their shallowness. Lectured on Locke to show them up. Except by the will of the majority, unambiguously expressed, there was no legitimate power. The only absolute democrat in America (perhaps in the world—although who can know what there is in the world, among so many billions of minds and souls) was Willis Mosby. Notwithstanding his terse, dry, intolerant style of conversation (more precisely, examination), his lank dignity of person, his aristocratic bones. Dark long nostrils hinting at the afflictions that needed the strength you could see in his jaws. And, finally, the light-pained eyes.

A most peculiar, ingenious, hungry, aspiring, and heart-broken animal, who, by calling himself Man, thinks he can escape being what he really is. Not a matter of his definition, in the last analysis, but of his being. Let him say what he likes.

> Kingdoms are clay: our dungy earth alike
> Feeds beast as man; the nobleness of life
> Is to do thus.

Thus being love. Or any other sublime option. (Mosby knew his Shakespeare anyway. *There* was a difference from the President. And of the Vice-President he said, "I wouldn't trust him to make me a pill. A has-been druggist!")

With sober lips he sipped the mescal, the servant in the coarse orange shirt enriched by metal buttons reminding him that the car was coming at four o'clock to take him to Mitla, to visit the ruins.

"*Yo mismo soy una ruina*," Mosby joked.

The stout Indian, giving only so much of a smile—no more—withdrew with quiet courtesy. Perhaps I was fishing, Mosby considered. Wanted him to say I was *not* a ruin. But how could he? Seeing that for him I *am* one.

Perhaps Mosby did not have a light touch. Still, he thought he did have an eye for certain kinds of comedy. And he *must* find a way to relieve the rigor of this account of his mental wars. Besides, he could really remember that in Paris at that time people, one after another, revealed themselves in a comic light. He was then seeing things that way. Rue Jacob, Rue Bonaparte, Rue du Bac, Rue de Verneuil, Hôtel de l'Université—filled with funny people.

He began by setting down a name: Lustgarten. Yes, there was the man he wanted. Hymen Lustgarten, a Marxist, or former Marxist, from New Jersey. From Newark, I think. He had been a shoe salesman, and belonged to any number of heretical, fanatical, bolshevistic groups. He had been a Leninist, a Trotskyist, then a follower of Hugo Oehler, then of Thomas Stamm, and finally of an Italian named Salemme who gave up politics to become a painter, an abstractionist. Lustgarten also gave up politics. He wanted now to be successful in business—rich. Believing that the nights he had spent poring over *Das Kapital* and Lenin's *State and Revolution* would give him an edge in business dealings. We were staying in the same hotel. I couldn't at first make out what he and his wife were doing. Presently I understood. The black market. This was not then reprehensible. Postwar Europe was like that. Refugees, adventurers, G.I.s. Even the Comte de la M.-C. Europe still shuddering from the blows it had received. Governments new, uncertain, infirm. No reason to respect their authority. American soldiers led the way. Flamboyant business schemes. Machines, whole factories, stolen, treasures shipped home. An American colonel in the lumber business started to saw up the Black Forest and send it to Wisconsin. And, of course, Nazis concealing their concentration-camp loot. Jewels sunk in Austrian lakes. Art works hidden. Gold extracted from teeth in extermination camps, melted into ingots and mortared like bricks into the walls of houses. Incredibly huge fortunes to be made, and Lustgarten intended to make one of them. Unfortunately, he was incompetent.

You could see at once that there was no harm in him. Despite the bold revolutionary associations, and fierceness of doctrine. Theoretical willingness to slay class enemies. But Lustgarten could not even hold his own with pushy people in a *pissoir*. Strangely meek, stout, swarthy, kindly, grinning with mulberry lips, a froggy, curving mouth which produced wrinkles like gills between the ears and the grin. And perhaps, Mosby thought, he comes to mind in Mexico because of his Toltec, Mixtec, Zapotec look, squat and black-haired, the tip of his nose turned downward and the black nostrils shyly widening when his friendly smile was accepted. And a bit sick with the wickedness, the awfulness of life but, respectfully persistent, bound to get his share. Efficiency was his style—action, determination, but a traitorous incompetence trembled within. Wrong calling. Wrong choice. A bad mistake. But he was persistent.

His conversation amused me, in the dining room. He was proud of his revolutionary activities, which had consisted mainly of cranking the mimeograph machine. Internal Bulletins. Thousands of pages of recondite examination of fine points of doctrine for the membership. Whether the American working class should give *material* aid to the Loyalist Government of Spain, controlled as that was by Stalinists and other class enemies and traitors. You had to fight Franco, and you had to fight Stalin as well. There was, of course, no material aid to give. But *had* there been any, *should* it have been given? This purely theoretical problem caused splits and expulsions. I always kept myself informed of these curious agonies of sectarianism, Mosby wrote. The single effort made by Spanish Republicans to purchase arms in the United States was thwarted by that friend of liberty Franklin Delano Roosevelt, who allowed one ship, the *Mar Cantábrico,* to be loaded but set the Coast Guard after it to turn it back to port. It was, I believe, that *genius* of diplomacy, Mr. Cordell Hull, who was responsible, but the decision, of course, was referred to F.D.R., whom Huey Long amusingly called Franklin de la *No!* But perhaps the most refined of these internal discussions left of left, the documents for which were turned out on the machine by that Jimmy Higgins, the tubby devoted party-worker Mr. Lustgarten, had to do with the Finnish War. Here the painful point of doctrine to be resolved was whether a Workers' State like the Soviet Union, even if it was a *degenerate* Workers' State, a product of the Thermidorian Reaction following the glorious Proletarian Revolution of 1917, could wage an Imperialistic War. For only the *bourgeoisie* could be Imperialistic. Technically, Stalinism could not be Imperialism. By definition. What then should a Revolutionary Party say to the Finns? Should they resist Russia or nòt? The Russians were monsters but they would expropriate the Mannerheim White-Guardist landowners and move, painful though it might be, in the correct historical direction. This, as a sect-watcher, I greatly relished. But it was too foreign a subtlety for many of the sectarians. Who were, after all, Americans. Pragmatists at heart. It was *too* far out for Lustgarten. He decided, after the war, to become (it shouldn't be hard) a rich man. Took his savings and, I believe his wife said, his mother's savings, and went abroad to build a fortune.

Within a year he had lost it all. He was cheated. By a German partner, in particular. But also he was caught smuggling by Belgian authorities.

When Mosby met him (Mosby speaking of himself in the third person as Henry Adams had done in *The Education of Henry Adams*)—when Mosby met him, Lustgarten was working for the American Army, employed by Graves Registration. Something to do with the procurement of crosses. Or with supervision of the lawns. Official employment gave Lustgarten PX privileges. He was rebuilding his financial foundations by the illegal sale of cigarettes. He dealt also in gas-ration coupons which the French Government, anxious to obtain dollars, would give you if you exchanged your money at the legal rate. The gas coupons were sold on the black market. The Lustgartens, husband and wife, persuaded Mosby to do this once. For them, he cashed his dollars at the bank, not with la Mine-Crevée. The occasion seemed important. Mosby gathered that Lustgarten had to drive at once to Munich. He had gone into the dental-supply business there with a German dentist who now denied that they had ever been partners.

Many consultations between Lustgarten (in his international intriguer's trenchcoat, ill-fitting; head, neck, and shoulders sloping backward in a froggy curve) and his wife, a young woman in an eyelet-lace blouse and black velveteen skirt, a velveteen ribbon tied on her round, healthy neck. Lustgarten, on the circular floor of the bank, explaining as they stood apart. And sweating blood; being reasonable with Trudy, detail by tortuous detail. It grated away poor Lustgarten's patience. Hands feebly remonstrating. For she asked female questions or raised objections which gave him agonies of patient rationality. Only there was nothing rational to begin with. That is, he had had no legal right to go into business with the German. All such arrangements had to be licensed by the Military Government. It was a black-market partnership and when it began to show a profit, the German threw Lustgarten out. With what they call impunity. Germany as a whole having discerned the limits of all civilized systems of punishment as compared with the unbounded possibilities of crime. The bank in Paris, where these explanations between Lustgarten and Trudy were taking place, had an interior of some sort of red porphyry. Like raw meat. A color which bourgeois France seemed to have vested with ideas of potency, mettle, and grandeur. In the Invalides also, Napoleon's sarcophagus was of polished red stone, a great, swooping, polished cradle containing the little green corpse. (We have the testimony of M. Rideau, the Bonapartist historian, as to the color.) As for the living Bonaparte, Mosby felt, with Auguste Comte, that he had been an anachronism. The Revolution was historically necessary. It was socially justified. Politically, economically, it was a move toward industrial democracy. But the Napoleonic drama itself belonged to an archaic category of personal ambitions, feudal ideas of war. Older than feudalism. Older than Rome. The commander at the head of armies—nothing rational to recommend it. Society, increasingly rational in its organization, did not need it. But humankind evidently desired it. War is a luxurious pleasure. Grant the first premise of hedonism and you must accept the rest also. Rational foundations of modernity are cunningly accepted by man as the launching platform of ever wilder irrationalities.

Mosby, writing these reflections in a blue-green color of ink which might have been extracted from the landscape. As his liquor had been extracted from the green spikes of the mescal, the curious sharp, dark-green fleshy limbs of the plant covering the fields.

The dollars, the francs, the gas rations, the bank like the beefsteak mine in which W. C. Fields invested, and shrinking but persistent dark Lustgarten getting into his little car on the sodden Parisian street. There were few cars then in Paris. Plenty of parking space. And the streets were so yellow, gray, wrinkled, dismal. But the French were even then ferociously telling the world that they had the *savoir-vivre*, the *gai savoir*. Especially Americans, haunted by their Protestant Ethic, had to hear this. My God—sit down, sip wine, taste cheese, break bread, hear music, know love, stop running, and learn ancient life-wisdom from Europe.

At anyrate, Lustgarten buckled up his trenchcoat, pulled down his big hoodlum's fedora. He was bunched up in the seat. Small brown hands holding the steering wheel of the Simca huit, and the grinning despair with which he waved.

"*Bonvoyage*, Lustgarten."

His Zapotec nose, his teeth like white pomegranate seeds. With a sob of the gears he took off for devastated Germany.

Reconstruction is big business. You demolish a society, you decrease the population, and off you go again. New fortunes. Lustgarten may have felt, *qua* Jew, that he had a right to grow rich in the German boom. That all Jews had natural claims beyond the Rhine. On land enriched by Jewish ashes. And you never could be sure, seated on a sofa, that it was not stuffed or upholstered with Jewish hair. And he would not use German soap. He washed his hands, Trudy told Mosby, with Lifebuoy from the PX.

Trudy, a graduate of Montclair Teachers' College in New Jersey, knew French, studied composition, had hoped to work with someone like Nadia Boulanger, but was obliged to settle for less. From the bank, as Lustgarten drove away in a kind of doomed, latently tearful daring in the rain-drenched street, Trudy invited Mosby to the Salle Pleyel, to hear a Czech pianist performing Schönberg. This man, with muscular baldness, worked very hard upon the keys. The difficulty of his enterprise alone came through—the labor of culture, the trouble it took to preserve art in tragic Europe, the devoted drill. Trudy had a nice face for concerts. Her odor was agreeable. She shone. In the left half of her countenance, one eye kept wandering. Stone-hearted Mosby, making fun of flesh and blood, of these little humanities with their short inventories of bad and good. The poor Czech in his blazer with chased buttons and the muscles of his forehead rising in protest against *tabula rasa*—the bare skull.

Mosby could abstract himself on such occasions. Shut

out the piano. Continue thinking about Comte. Begone, old priests and feudal soldiers! Go, with Theology and Metaphysics! And in the Positive Epoch Enlightened Woman would begin to play her part, vigilant, preventing the managers of the new society from abusing their powers. Over Labor, the Supreme Good.

Embroidering the trees, the birds of Mexico, looking at Mosby, and the hummingbird, so neat in its lust, vibrating tinily, and the lizard on the soil drinking heat with its belly. To bless small creatures is supposed to be real good.

Yes, this Lustgarten was a funny man. Cheated in Germany, licked by the partner, and impatient with his slow progress in Graves Registration, he decided to import a Cadillac. Among the new postwar millionaires of Europe there was a big demand for Cadillacs. The French Government, moving slowly, had not yet taken measures against such imports for rapid resale. In 1947, no tax prevented such transactions. Lustgarten got his family in Newark to ship a new Cadillac. Something like four thousand dollars was raised by his brother, his mother, his mother's brother for the purpose. The car was sent. The customer was waiting. A down payment had already been given. A double profit was expected. Only, on the day the car was unloaded at Le Havre new regulations went into effect. The Cadillac could not be sold. Lustgarten was stuck with it. He couldn't even afford to buy gas. The Lustgartens were seen one day moving out of the hotel, into the car. Mrs. Lustgarten went to live with musical friends. Mosby offered Lustgarten the use of his sink for washing and shaving. Weary Lustgarten, defeated, depressed, frightened at last by his own plunging, scraped at his bristles, mornings, with a modest cricket noise, while sighing. All that money—mother's savings, brother's pension. No wonder his eyelids turned blue. And his smile, like a spinster's sachet, the last fragrance ebbed out long ago in the trousseau never used. But the long batrachian lips continued smiling.

Mosby realized that compassion should be felt. But passing in the night the locked, gleaming car, and seeing huddled Lustgarten, sleeping, covered with two coats, on the majestic seat, like Jonah inside Leviathan, Mosby could not say in candor that what he experienced was sympathy. Rather he reflected that this shoe salesman, in America attached to foreign doctrines, who could not relinquish Europe in the New World, was now, in Paris, sleeping in the Cadillac, encased in this gorgeous Fisher Body from Detroit. At home exotic, in Europe a Yankee. His timing was off. He recognized this himself. But believed, in general, that he was too early. A pioneer. For instance, he said, in a voice that creaked with shy assertiveness, the French were only now beginning to be Marxians. He had gone through it all years ago. What did these people know! Ask them about the Shakhty Engineers! About Lenin's Democratic Centralism! About the Moscow Trials! About "Social Fascism"! They were ignorant. The Revolution having been totally betrayed, these Europeans suddenly discovered Marx and Lenin. "Eureka!" he said in a high voice. And it was the Cold War, beneath it all. For should America lose, the French intellectuals were preparing to collaborate with Russia. And should America win they could still be free, defiant radicals under American protection.

"You sound like a patriot," said Mosby.

"Well, in a way I am," said Lustgarten. "But I am getting to be objective. Sometimes I say to myself, 'If you were outside the world, if you, Lustgarten, didn't exist as a man, what would your opinion be of this or that?' "

"Disembodied truth."

"I guess that's what it is."

"And what are you going to do about the Cadillac?" said Mosby.

"I'm sending it to Spain. We can sell it in Barcelona."

"But you have to get it there."

"Through Andorra. It's all arranged. Klonsky is driving it."

Klonsky was a Polish Belgian in the hotel. One of Lustgarten's associates, congenitally dishonest, Mosby thought. Kinky hair, wrinkled eyes like Greek olives, and a cat nose and cat lips. He wore Russian boots.

But no sooner had Klonsky departed for Andorra, than Lustgarten received a marvelous offer for the car. A capitalist in Utrecht wanted it at once and would take care of all excise problems. He had all the necessary *tuyaux*, unlimited drag. Lustgarten wired Klonsky in Andorra to stop. He raced down on the night train, recovered the Cadillac, and started driving back at once. There was no time to lose. But after sitting up all night on the *rapide*, Lustgarten was drowsy in the warmth of the Pyrenees and fell asleep at the wheel. He was lucky, he later said, for the car went down a mountainside and might have missed the stone wall that stopped it. He was only a foot or two from death when he was awakened by the crash. The car was destroyed. It was not insured.

Still faintly smiling, Lustgarten, with his sling and cane, came to Mosby's café table on the Boulevard Saint-Germain. Sat down. Removed his hat from dazzling black hair. Asked permission to rest his injured foot on a chair. "Is this a private conversation?" he said.

Mosby had been chatting with Alfred Ruskin, an American poet. Ruskin, though some of his front teeth were missing, spoke very clearly and swiftly. A perfectly charming man. Inveterately theoretical. He had been saying, for instance, that France had shot its collaborationist poets. America, which had no poets to spare, put Ezra Pound in Saint Elizabeth's. He then went on to say, barely acknowledging Lustgarten, that America had had no history, was not a historical society. His proof was from Hegel. According to Hegel, history was the history of wars and revolutions. The United States had had only one revolution and very few wars. Therefore it was historically empty. Practically a vacuum.

Ruskin also used Mosby's conveniences at the hotel, being too fastidious for his own latrine in the Algerian back streets of the Left Bank. And when he emerged from the bathroom he invariably had a topic sentence.

"I have discovered the main defect of Kierkegaard."

Or, "Pascal was terrified by universal emptiness, but Valéry says the difference between empty space and space in a bottle is only quantitative, and there is nothing intrinsically terrifying about quantity. What is your view?"

We do not live in bottles—Mosby's reply.

Lustgarten said when Ruskin left us, "Who is that fellow? He mooched you for the coffee."

"Ruskin," said Mosby.

"*That* is Ruskin?"

"Yes, why?"

"I hear my wife was going out with Ruskin while I was in the hospital."

"Oh, I wouldn't believe such rumors," said Mosby. "A cup of coffee, an apéritif together, maybe."

"When a man is down on his luck," said Lustgarten, "it's the rare woman who won't give him hell in addition."

"Sorry to hear it," Mosby replied.

And then, as Mosby in Oaxaca recalled, shifting his seat from the sun—for he was already far too red, and his face, bones, eyes, seemed curiously thirsty—Lustgarten had said, "It's been a terrible experience."

"Undoubtedly so, Lustgarten. It must have been frightening."

"What crashed was my last stake. It involved family. Too bad in a way that I wasn't killed. My insurance would at least have covered my kid brother's loss. And my mother and uncle."

Mosby had no wish to see a man in tears. He did not care

to sit through these moments of suffering. Such unmastered emotion was abhorrent. Though perhaps the violence of this abomination might have told Mosby something about his own moral constitution. Perhaps Lustgarten did not want his face to be working. Or tried to subdue his agitation, seeing from Mosby's austere, though not unkind, silence that this was not his way. Mosby was by taste a Senecan. At least he admired Spanish masculinity—the *varonil* of Lorca. The *clavel varonil*, the manly red carnation, the clear classic hardness of honorable control.

"You sold the wreck for junk, I assume?"

"Klonksy took care of it. Now look, Mosby. I'm through with that. I was reading, thinking, in the hospital. I came over to make a pile. Like the gold rush. I really don't know what got into me. Trudy and I were just sitting around during the war. I was too old for the draft. And we both wanted action. She in music. Or life. Excitement. You know, dreaming at Montclair Teachers' College of the Big Time. I wanted to make it possible for her. Keep up with the world, or something. But really—in my hospital bed I realized—I was right the first time. I am a socialist. A natural idealist. Reading about Attlee, I felt at home again. It became clear that I am still a political animal."

Mosby wished to say, "No, Lustgarten. You're a dandler of swarthy little babies. You're a piggyback man—a giddyap horsie. You're a sweet old Jewish Daddy." But he said nothing.

"And I also read," said Lustgarten, "about Tito. Maybe the Tito alternative is the real one. Perhaps there is hope for socialism somewhere between the Labour Party and the Yugoslav type of leadership. I feel it my duty," Lustgarten told Mosby, "to investigate. I'm thinking of going to Belgrade."

"As what?"

"As a matter of fact, that's where you could come in," said Lustgarten. "If you would be so kind. You're not *just* a scholar. You wrote a book on Plato, I've been told."

"On the *Laws*."

"And other books. But in addition you know the Movement. Lots of people. More connections than a switchboard. . . ."

The slang of the forties.

"You know people at the *New Leader*?"

"Not my type of paper," said Mosby. "I'm actually a political conservative. Not what you would call a Rotten Liberal but an out-and-out conservative. I shook Franco's hand, you know."

"Did you?"

"This very hand shook the hand of the Caudillo. Would you like to touch it for yourself?"

"Why should I?"

"Go on," said Mosby. "It may mean something. Shake the hand that shook the hand."

Very strangely, then, Lustgarten extended padded, swarthy fingers. He looked partly subtle, partly ill. Grinning, he said, "Now I've made contact with real politics at last. But I'm serious about the *New Leader*. You probably know Bohn. I need credentials for Yugoslavia."

"Have you ever written for the papers?"

"For the *Militant*."

"What did you write?"

Guilty Lustgarten did not lie well. It was heartless of Mosby to amuse himself in this way.

"I have a scrapbook somewhere," said Lustgarten.

But it was not necessary to write to the *New Leader*. Lustgarten, encountered two days later on the Boulevard, near the pork butcher, had taken off the sling and scarcely needed the cane. He said, "I'm going to Yugoslavia. I've been invited."

"By whom?"

"Tito. The Government. They're asking interested people to come as guests to tour the country and see how they're building socialism. Oh, I know," he quickly said, anticipating standard doctrinal objection, "you don't build socialism in one country, but it's no longer the same situation. And I really believe Tito may redeem Marxism by actually transforming the dictatorship of the proletariat. This brings me back to my first love—the radical movement. I was never meant to be an entrepreneur."

"Probably not."

"I feel some hope," Lustgarten shyly said. "And then also, it's getting to be spring." He was wearing his heavy moose-colored bristling hat, and bore many other signs of interminable winter. A candidate for resurrection. An opportunity for the grace of life to reveal itself. But perhaps, Mosby thought, a man like Lustgarten would never, except with supernatural aid, exist in a suitable form.

"Also," said Lustgarten touchingly, "this will give Trudy time to reconsider."

"Is that the way things are with you two? I'm sorry."

"I wish I could take her with me, but I can't swing that with the Yugoslavs. It's sort of a V.I.P. deal. I guess they want to affect foreign radicals. There'll be seminars in dialectics, and so on. I love it. But it's not Trudy's dish."

Steady-handed, Mosby on his patio took ice with tongs, and poured more mescal flavored with *gusano de maguey*— a worm or slug of delicate flavor. These notes on Lustgarten pleased him. It was essential, at this point in his memoirs, to disclose new depths. The preceding chapters had been heavy. Many unconventional things were said about the state of political theory. The weakness of conservative doctrine, the lack, in America, of conservative alternatives, of resistance to the prevailing liberalism. As one who had personally tried to create a more rigorous environment for slovenly intellectuals, to force them to do their homework, to harden the categories of political thought, he was aware that on the right as on the left the results were barren. Absurdly, the college-bred dunces of America had longed for a true left wing movement on the European model.

They still dreamed of it. No less absurd were the right-wing idiots. You cannot grow a rose in a coal mine. Mosby's own right-wing graduate students had disappointed him. Just a lot of television actors. Bad guys for the Susskind interview programs. They had transformed the master's manner of acid elegance, logical tightness, factual punctiliousness, and merciless laceration in debate into a sort of shallow Noël Coward style. The real, the original Mosby approach brought Mosby hatred, got Mosby fired. Princeton University had offered Mosby a lump sum to retire seven years early. One hundred and forty thousand dollars. Because his mode of discourse was so upsetting to the academic community. Mosby was invited to no television programs. He was like the Guerrilla Mosby of the Civil War. When he galloped in, all were slaughtered.

Most carefully, Mosby had studied the memoirs of Santayana, Malraux, Sartre, Lord Russell, and others. Unfortunately, no one was reliably or consistently great. Men whose lives had been devoted to thought, who had tried mightily to govern the disorder of public life, to put it under some sort of intellectual authority, to get ideas to save mankind or to offer it mental aid in saving itself, would suddenly turn into gruesome idiots. Wanting to kill everyone. For instance, Sartre calling for the Russians to drop A-bombs on American bases in the Pacific because America was now presumably monstrous. And exhorting the blacks to butcher the whites. This moral philosopher! Or Russell, the Pacifist of World War I, urging the West to annihilate Russia after World War II. And sometimes, in his memoirs—perhaps he was gaga—strangely illogical. When, over London, a Zeppelin was shot down, the bodies of Germans were seen to fall, and the brutal men in the street horribly cheered, Russell wept, and had there not been a beautiful woman to console him in bed that night, this heartlessness of mankind would have broken him utterly. What was omitted was the fact that these same Germans who fell from the Zeppelin had come to bomb the city. They were going to blow up the brutes in the street, explode the lovers. This Mosby saw.

It was earnestly to be hoped—this was the mescal attempting to invade his language—that Mosby would avoid the common fate of intellectuals. The Lustgarten digression should help. The correction of pride by laughter.

There were twenty minutes yet before the chauffeur came to take the party to Mitla, to the ruins. Mosby had time to continue. To say that in September the Lustgarten who reappeared looked frightful. He had lost no less than fifty pounds. Sun-blackened, creased, in a filthy stained suit, his eyes infected. He said he had had diarrhea all summer.

"What did they feed their foreign V.I.P.s?"

And Lustgarten shyly bitter—the lean face and inflamed eyes materializing from a spiritual region very different from any heretofore associated with Lustgarten by Mosby—said, "It was just a chain gang. It was hard labor. I didn't understand the deal. I thought we were invited, as I told you. But we turned out to be foreign volunteers-of-construction. A labor brigade. And up in the mountains. Never saw the Dalmatian coast. Hardly even shelter for the night. We slept on the ground and ate shit fried in rancid oil."

"Why didn't you run away?" asked Mosby.

"How? Where?"

"Back to Belgrade. To the American Embassy at least?"

"How could I? I was a guest. Came at their expense. They held the return ticket."

"And no money?"

"Are you kidding? Dead broke. In Macedonia. Near Skoplje. Bug-stung, starved, and running to the latrine all night. Laboring on the roads all day, with pus in my eyes, too."

"No first aid?"

"They may have had the first, but they didn't have the second."

Mosby though it best to say nothing of Trudy. She had divorced Lustgarten.

Commiseration, of course.

Mosby shaking his head.

Lustgarten with a certain skinny dignity walking away. He himself seemed amused by his encounters with Capitalism and Socialism.

The end? Not quite. There was a coda: The thing had quite good form.

Lustgarten and Mosby met again. Five years later. Mosby enters an elevator in New York. Express to the forty-seventh floor, the executive dining room of the Rangeley Foundation. There is one other passenger, and it is Lustgarten. Grinning. He is himself again, filled out once more.

"Lustgarten!"

"Willis Mosby!"

"How are you, Lustgarten?"

"I'm great. Things are completely different. I'm happy. Successful. Married. Children."

"In New York?"

"Wouldn't live in the U.S. again. It's godawful. Inhuman. I'm visiting."

Without a blink in its brilliancy, without a hitch in its smooth, regulated power, the elevator containing only the two of us was going up. The same Lustgarten. Strong words, vocal insufficiency, the Zapotec nose, and under it the frog smile, the kindly gills.

"Where are you going now?"

"Up to *Fortune*," said Lustgarten. "I want to sell them a story."

He was on the wrong elevator. This one was not going to *Fortune*. I told him so. Perhaps I had not changed either. A voice which for many years had informed people of their errors said, "You'll have to go down again. The other bank of elevators."

At the forty-seventh floor we emerged together.

"Where are you settled now?"

"In Algiers," said Lustgarten. "We have a laundromat there."

"We?"

"Klonsky and I. You remember Klonsky?"

They had gone legitimate. They were washing burnooses. He was married to Klonsky's sister. I saw her picture. The image of Klonsky, a cat-faced woman, head ferociously encased in kinky hair, Picasso eyes at different levels, sharp teeth. If fish, dozing in the reefs, had nightmares, they would be of such teeth. The children also were young Klonskys. Lustgarten had the snapshots in his wallet of North African leather. As he beamed, Mosby recognized that pride in his success was Lustgarten's opiate, his artificial paradise.

"I thought," said Lustgarten, "that *Fortune* might like a piece on how we made it in North Africa."

We then shook hands again. Mine the hand that had shaken Franco's hand—his that had slept on the wheel of the Cadillac. The lighted case opened for him. He entered in. It shut.

Thereafter, of course, the Algerians threw out the French, expelled the Jews. And Jewish-Daddy-Lustgarten must have moved on. Passionate fatherhood. He loved those children. For Plato this child-breeding is the lowest level of creativity.

Still, Mosby thought, under the influence of mescal, my parents begot me like a committee of two.

From a feeling of remotion, though he realized that the car for Mitla had arrived, a shining conveyance waited, he noted the following as he gazed at the afternoon mountains:

Until he was some years old
People took care of him
Cooled his soup, sang, chirked,
Drew on his long stockings,
Carried him upstairs sleeping.
He recalls at the green lakeside
His father's solemn navel,
Nipples like dog's eyes in the hair
Mother's thigh with wisteria of blue veins.

After they retired to death,
He conducted his own business
Not too modestly, not too well.
But here he is, smoking in Mexico
Considering the brown mountains
Whose fat laps are rolling
On the skulls of whole families.

Two Welsh women were his companions. One was very ancient, lank. The Wellington of lady travelers. Or like C. Aubrey Smith, the actor who used to command Gurkha regiments in movies about India. A great nose, a gaunt jaw, a pleated lip, a considerable mustache. The other was younger. She had a small dewlap, but her cheeks were round and dark eyes witty. A very satisfactory pair. Decent was the word. English traits. Like many Americans, Mosby desired such traits for himself. Yes, he was pleased with the Welsh ladies. Though the guide was unsuitable. Overweening. His fat cheeks a red pottery color. And he drove too fast.

The first stop was at Tule. They got out to inspect the celebrated Tule tree in the churchyard. This monument of vegetation, intricately and densely convolved, a green cypress, more than two thousand years old, roots in a vanished lake bottom, older than the religion of this little heap of white and gloom, this charming peasant church. In the comfortable dust, a dog slept. Disrespectful. But unconscious. The old lady, quietly dauntless, tied on a scarf and entered the church. Her stiff genuflection had real quality. She must be Christian. Mosby looked into the depths of the Tule. A world in itself! It could contain communities. In fact, if he recalled his Gerald Heard, there was supposed to be a primal tree occupied by early ancestors, the human horde housed in such appealing, dappled, commodious, altogether beautiful organisms. The facts seemed not to support this golden myth of an encompassing paradise. Earliest man probably ran about on the ground, horribly violent, killing everything. Still, this dream of gentleness, this aspiration for arboreal peace was no small achievement for the descendants of so many killers. For his religion, this tree would do, thought Mosby. No church for him.

He was sorry to go. *He* could have lived up there. On top, of course. The excrements would drop on you below. But the Welsh ladies were already in the car, and the bossy guide began to toot the horn. Waiting was hot.

The road to Mitla was empty. The heat made the landscape beautifully crooked. The driver knew geology, archaeology. He was quite ugly with his information. The Water Table, the Caverns, the Triassic Period. Inform me no further! Vex not my soul with more detail. I cannot use what I have! And now Mitla appeared. The right fork continued to Tehuantepec. The left brought you to the Town of Souls. Old Mrs. Parsons (Elsie Clews Parsons, as Mosby's mental retrieval system told him) had done ethnography here, studied the Indians in these baked streets of adobe and fruit garbage. In the shade, a dark urinous tang. A long-legged pig struggling on a tether. A sow. From behind, observant Mosby identified its pink small female opening. The dungy earth feeding beast as man.

But here were the fascinating temples, almost intact. This place the Spanish priests had not destroyed. All others they had razed, building churches on the same sites, using the same stones.

A tourist market. Coarse cotton dresses, Indian embroidery, hung under flour-white tarpaulins, the dust settling on the pottery of the region, black saxophones, black trays of glazed clay.

Following the British travelers and the guide, Mosby was going once more through an odd and complex fantasy. It was that he was dead. He had died. He continued, however, to live. His doom was to live life to the end as Mosby. In the fantasy, he considered this his purgatory. And when had death occurred? In a collision years ago. He had thought it a near thing then. The cars were demolished. The actual Mosby was killed. But another Mosby was pulled from the car. A trooper asked, "You okay?"

Yes, he was okay. Walked away from the wreck. But he still had the whole thing to do, step by step, moment by moment. And now he heard a parrot blabbing, and children panhandled him and women made their pitch, and he was getting his shoes covered with dust. He had been working at his memoirs and had provided a diverting recollection of a funny man—Lustgarten. In the manner of Sir Harold Nicolson. Much less polished, admittedly, but in accordance with a certain protocol, the language of diplomacy, of mandarin irony. However certain facts had been omitted. Mosby had arranged, for instance, that Trudy should be seen with Alfred Ruskin. For when Lustgarten was crossing the Rhine, Mosby was embracing Trudy in bed. Unlike Lord Russell's beautiful friend, she did not comfort Mosby for the disasters he had (by intellectual commitment) to confront. But Mosby had not advised her about leaving Lustgarten. He did not mean to interfere. However, his vision of Lustgarten as a funny man was transmitted to Trudy. She could not be the wife of such a funny man. But he *was*, he *was* a funny man! He was, like Napoleon in the eyes of Comte, an anachronism. Inept, he wished to be a colossus, something of a Napoleon himself, make millions, conquer Europe, retrieve from Hitler's fall a colossal fortune. Poorly imagined, unoriginal, the rerun of old ideas, and so inefficient. Lustgarten didn't have to happen. And so he *was* funny. Trudy too was funny, however. What a large belly she had. Since individuals are sometimes born from a twin impregnation, the organism carrying the undeveloped brother or sister in vestigial form—at times no more than an extra organ, a rudimentary eye buried in the leg, or a kidney or the beginnings of an ear somewhere in the back—Mosby often thought that Trudy had a little sister inside her. And to him she was a clown. This need not mean contempt. No, he liked her. The eye seemed to wander in one hemisphere. She did not know how to use perfume. Her atonal compositions were foolish.

At this time, Mosby had been making fun of people.

"Why?"

"Because he had needed to."

"Why?"

"Because!"

The guide explained that the buildings were raised without mortar. The mathematical calculations of the priests had been perfect. The precision of the cut stone was absolute. After centuries you could not find a chink, you could not insert a razor blade anywhere. These geometrical masses were balanced by their own weight. Here the priests lived. The walls had been dyed. The cochineal or cactus louse provided the dye. Here were the altars. Spectators sat where you are standing. The priests used obsidian knives. The beautiful youths played on flutes. Then the flutes were broken. The bloody knife was wiped on the head of the executioner. Hair must have been clotted. And here, the tombs of the nobles. Stairs leading down. The Zapotecs, late in the day, had practiced this form of sacrifice, under Aztec influence.

How game this Welsh crone was. She was beautiful. Getting in and out of these pits, she required no assistance.

Of course you cannot make yourself an agreeable, desirable person. You can't will yourself into it without regard to the things to be done. Imperative tasks. Imperative comprehensions, monstrous compulsions of duty which deform. Men will grow ugly under such necessities. This one a director of espionage. That one a killer.

Mosby had evoked, to lighten the dense texture of his memoirs, a Lustgarten whose doom was this gaping comedy. A Lustgarten who didn't have to happen. But himself, Mosby, also a separate creation, a finished product, standing under the sun on large blocks of stone, on the stairs descending into this pit, he was complete. He had completed himself in this cogitating, unlaughing, stone, iron, nonsensical form.

Having disposed of all things human, he should have encountered God.

Would this occur?

But having so disposed, what God was there to encounter?

But they had now been led below, into the tomb. There was a heavy grille, the gate. The stones were huge. The vault was close. He was oppressed. He was afraid. It was very damp. On the elaborately zigzag-carved walls were thin, thin pipings of fluorescent light. Flat boxes of ground lime were here to absorb moisture. His heart was paralyzed. His lungs would not draw. Jesus! I cannot catch my breath! To be shut in here! To be dead here! Suppose one were! Not as in accidents which ended, but did not quite end, existence. *Dead*-dead. Stooping, he looked for daylight. Yes, it was there. The light was there. The grace of life still there. Or, if not grace, air. Go while you can.

"I must get out," he told the guide. "Ladies, I find it very hard to breathe."